Logan Bruno, Boy Baby-sitter

Logan Bruno, Boy Baby-sitter

Ann M. Martin

AN
APPLE
PAPERBACK

SCHOLASTIC INC.
New York Toronto London Auckland Sydney

Cover art by Hodges Soileau

Twister ® is a registered trademark of Milton Bradley Co.,
a Division of Hasbro, Inc. Used with permission.

ISBN 0-590-47118-X

Copyright © 1993 by Ann M. Martin. All rights reserved. Published
by Scholastic Inc. APPLE PAPERBACKS ® and THE BABY-SITTERS
CLUB ® are registered trademarks of Scholastic Inc.

12 11 10 9 8 7 6 5 4 3 2 1   3 4 5 6 7 8/9

Printed in the U.S.A.   40

First Scholastic printing, July 1993

*The author gratefully acknowledges
Peter Lerangis
for his help in
preparing this manuscript.*

CHAPTER 1

"**M**ore syrup on my waffles!" cried my brother Hunter. (Actually he is the Prince of Allergies, so it came out more like "Bo syrup odd by waffles!")

"Hrmmph . . . ?" grunted my dad as he sipped his coffee.

"*Pleeease!*" Hunter added quickly. "It all soaked in!"

Dad made a face. "Honey, is the half-and-half sour?" he asked my mother.

"No!" Mom said to Hunter. Then she sniffed the half-and-half carton. "Yes."

"No?" Dad repeated. "Funny. Could it be the coffee?"

Mom sighed. "I *said* — "

Bang! My sister Kerry slammed the door to the cereal cabinet. "Who ate all the Cheerios?"

"I did," Hunter said with a grin. "Yesterday."

"Pig!"

"*Mo-om*, Kerry called me a — "

"A little less noise, please," Dad said.

"We have corn flakes," Mom suggested.

"Ewwww, I'd rather eat cardboard!" Kerry wailed.

"Okay! I'll get some!" Hunter hopped off his chair.

"*Sit down!*" That was Mom, Dad, and Kerry in unison.

Welcome to the Bruno kitchen. It was seven AM on a typical Monday. Total chaos. What a way to begin the week.

Me? I was feeling as if I'd been run over by a truck.

Okay, here's the first thing you should know about me. I, Logan Bruno, am not a morning person. I'm a nice guy most of the day. But pre-breakfast? Forget it. Call me Draculogan.

Here are some things you should know about the *post*-breakfast me. I lose my fangs and become a pretty normal thirteen-year-old boy. I'm in eighth grade at Stoneybrook Middle School in Stoneybrook, Connecticut — but I grew up in Louisville, Kentucky. I guess I have an accent, but if you ask me, it's the people up North who talk funny (and way too fast). I like sports, but I'm not a hard-core jock. Which means I can walk and talk at the same time, and I don't carry a football to bed with me. (Well, *no* jocks are like that, really, but some people conjure up this stereotype . . .) I look pretty average, medium height with blue eyes and blondish brown hair. My girl-friend, Mary Anne Spier, says I look like the actor Cam Geary. I don't, exactly, but I just thought I'd say that so you don't think I look like Garth from *Wayne's World* or something.

Anyway, while we're on my favorite subject (Mary Anne, not Garth), I should mention I was supposed to meet her at seven-thirty at Brenner Field. I had almost forgotten.

"Morning," I said as I slipped into the kitchen. Quickly I poured myself some cereal and grabbed a banana.

"Morning," said Dad.

"Morning," said Mom.

"Morning," said Hunter.

"Ohhhhhh," said Kerry, slumping into her seat.

"You okay?" I asked.

She shook her head. "Uh-uh. I don't feel so good."

"What's wrong?" Mom asked.

"She's going to barf!" Hunter said happily. "Ew! Ew!"

"I am not!" Kerry snapped back. "I think I just need a little rest."

Dad raised a suspicious eyebrow. "I'll call Doctor Kahn and set up an appointment."

"No!" Kerry shot back.

I tried to look her in the eye, but she turned away. Aha! I, Dr. Bruno, could detect telltale signs of the Kerry Bruno Anti-School Virus.

She last had the "symptoms" when we moved to Stoneybrook. They would appear mysteriously every weekday morning. And they finally went away when Kerry began to make friends.

I felt bad for her that Monday. Something was bugging her, and she wasn't saying what it was. Mom and Dad were determined to make her go to school.

As for me, I decided to stay out of the fireworks. I scarfed down my breakfast, grabbed my backpack, and ran out the door.

" 'Bye!" I called out. "Good luck, Kerry!"

" 'Bye, Logan!" Hunter called back.

I jogged down Fawcett Avenue and across Brenner Field. I could see Mary Anne on the other side. She was wearing earphones and tapping her feet to some song. "Hi!" I yelled, and I broke into a sprint.

She took off the phones and started to applaud. As I got closer, she called out, "How can you do that?"

I put my arm around her shoulder. "Do what?"

"Run like that so early in the morning."

"Must be the pork chops I had for breakfast," I said. "Lots of protein."

"Gross!"

"At least I didn't fall down."

Mary Anne's brow crinkled. "Oh, Logan, you're still thinking about the meet, aren't you?"

Talk about sensitive. Mary Anne is incredible; sometimes she can tell what's on my mind before I say a word. It is definitely one of the coolest things about her, right up there with a great sense of humor, deep brown eyes, and the most amazing smile. Seriously, if you could take and bottle Mary Anne's smile, it could probably cure grouchiness throughout the world. I felt better just looking at her.

I know, I know, I sound corny when I start talking about Mary Anne. (Well, you would too, if she were your girlfriend. Nuff said.)

I guess I should tell you what Mary Anne was talking about. I'm on the SMS track team, and we'd had a meet that Saturday. Our opponent, Mercer Junior High, was ahead by a point going into the last event, the hundred-yard dash. Now, that's *my* event and I'm pretty good at it. In practice I had tied the county all-time record. I was all fired up to beat it.

I never reached the finish line. I fell. Just

flat-out tripped on my own feet. Too excited, I guess.

We lost the meet. I was pretty embarrassed. (Embarrassed? I felt like moving out of town.) Fortunately I had gotten over it by Monday.

I shrugged. "Nah, we didn't lose any ground in the standings. I'm not really thinking about it anymore."

"Okay . . ." Mary Anne didn't believe me. I could tell.

We began walking toward school, and I wanted to change the subject. "What were you listening to?"

"Nicky Cash," she said.

I should have known. Mary Anne had only been listening to that tape for weeks.

I told you she was sensitive, right? Well, here's an example. Nicky Cash is this teenage singer who records all these gooshy love songs. Mary Anne always cries when she listens to him. Now, if someone made you cry, wouldn't that be a reason *not* to listen to him anymore? I'd think so. But Mary Anne can't get enough of his songs.

To be honest, I can't understand what the big deal is. Nicky Cash doesn't have such a great voice. But he's a pretty good dancer and girls think he's cute. He used to be in this group called 2 Hot 4 U, but broke off as a solo act. Now he's the hottest ticket around. When a local radio station announced he was giving a concert in Stamford, the phone lines broke down from overuse. You can't even say his name without some girl squealing. Mary Anne insists he's talented. She says I'm biased because I'm a guy. (I say she's biased because she's a girl. You know how it is.)

You know what else? His real name is Reginald Fenster.

"I saw a display for his new disc at Sound Ideas," I said. "He's bare-chested on the cover." (See what a thoughtful boyfriend I am, mentioning stuff like this?)

I thought Mary Anne's eyes would pop out. "Ohhhh, I hope it doesn't sell out."

"I can ask Bob to hold one for you," I suggested.

"Bob, the guy who owns the store?"

"Yeah. He and my dad know each other from the Chamber of Commerce Softball League. He's always saving, like, oldies collections for Dad and giving us discounts."

"Really? Logan, that is so sweet!"

"As long as you promise never to play it when I'm around."

"I guess I won't be seeing much of you then," she said with a sly smile.

"Thanks a lot!"

"For your information," Mary Anne went on, "we took a poll at the last BSC meeting, and every single one of us thought he was truly talented."

I shrugged. "Of course. You're all girls."

"Lo-*gannn!*"

In case you don't know, BSC stands for Baby-sitters Club. Mary Anne is a member, and so are eight of her friends, including her stepsister Dawn. I'll tell you more about the BSC later.

Oh. Just so you know, I am technically one of those eight friends. Meaning I'm in the Baby-sitters Club. But as an *associate*. I only go to some of the meetings and take some sitting jobs. I can't be a full member, because of after-school sports.

Not that I would be a full member even if I could. It's a lot of work. And since all the other members are girls, sometimes I feel a little weird in the meetings. *They* don't feel free to talk about all their usual stuff. *I* end up smiling a lot for no reason and looking at the clock.

I mean, there's nothing *wrong* with being a full member. Guys do make good baby-sitters. Sometimes even better than girls, in my opinion. Saying a guy can't sit is like saying a girl can't play football or hockey. A dumb stereotype. And hey, I *like* kids. And I like the BSC members. So why *shouldn't* I belong to the club? Big deal, right? It's no crime.

Whoa, calm down, Bruno.

Sorry. As you can see, I get kind of carried away on this subject. Being a boy baby-sitter isn't easy. Some of my track teammates find the idea hilarious. They think sitting is one step away from major sissyhood. Don't ask me why. Once I had to fill in temporarily for a BSC member who went to California. It was during football season, so I ended up missing some practices. You wouldn't believe the insults that started flying. Eventually the guys backed off, but things were never quite the same.

"Yo, potty animal! What's up?"

Zing. See what I mean? It was starting again. Insult Number One of the day was launched from the steps of SMS by Clarence King.

I could feel Mary Anne's hand clenching in mine. "Here he goes again," she murmured.

"He's just being his usual self," I said. Forcing a smile, I called out, "Hey, King, what's up?"

King is a member of the track team. He's huge. He's loud. He's a good athlete. And he's a big pain in the neck when he wants to be.

"Nice morning, huh?" he said with a grin. He began striding toward us, chest puffed out, right hand extended for a handshake.

Then he plunged to the ground. His comic books went flying. "Oops! Must have tripped over my own feet! Sorry!"

Really subtle, huh? King was doing an imitation of me at the meet on Saturday.

The guys behind him were cracking up. A couple of them, Peter Hayes and Irv Hirsch, are also members of the track team.

"Watch where you trip," I said. "I walked my dog there this morning."

King sprang to his feet and looked down.

"Rank!" I said. (Okay, so I sink to his level. Sometimes it's the only thing to do.)

"I knew you were kidding," King replied, trying to look suave. "Hey, I was just kidding, too. Don't look at me like that, Mary Anne."

Mary Anne was silent. Her face was a storm cloud. We walked into school, leaving a chorus of snickering behind us.

"He is so cruel," she said.

"Yeah," I replied. "But sensitive and warm underneath, and very willing to help me with my homework."

Mary Anne clapped her hand over her mouth, trying not to laugh. She does that sometimes, as if someone will get mad at her for letting out a big "HA!"

Oh, well, at least I managed to lighten things up. Mary Anne and I said good-bye and went to our lockers, which are in two different directions.

On the way, I started thinking about what

10

King had said. And where he had said it. And who he had said it in front of.

I thought he had changed. I was wrong.

In football, you learn to find your opponent's weakest spot, then attack that spot with all your strength. Well, that's what King was doing. He acted as if he'd been *waiting* for me to make a mistake. And now that I'd messed up, he was going to attack until I gave in.

And as usual, he was going to try to turn everyone else against me.

All because of that one stupid track meet. Was that infantile or what? What kind of friends were these, anyway?

As I turned the corner to my locker, I passed a group of guys huddled by a side door of the school. Each of them was wearing a black leather jacket with a symbol drawn on the back: two eyes, angry and bloodshot, with a dagger underneath, slicing through the letters *BB*.

The Badd Boyz.

I'm serious. That's what these guys call themselves. They're the junior version of a high school gang. They like to hang out in the shadows of the school, looking bored. Sometimes they smoke cigarettes, sometimes they work on the cars belonging to the older gang members. But mostly they spend their time trying to look cool. You'd be surprised how many guys look up to them, even a few of the goody-goody ones. And some girls treat them like movie stars. Then there are kids who insist the Badd Boyz are criminals: they say they steal cars, break into houses, hold up kids for pocket money, things like that.

Personally, I never believed a word of those horror stories. I also didn't think these guys were heroes. They just like to put on a dangerous image. I knew a couple of the Badd Boyz from my classes, and they seemed okay.

Anyway, I kind of nodded at them and headed to my locker.

"Hey, Bruno," I heard someone call.

I turned around. The Badd Boyz were glaring at me. One of their leaders, a guy named T-Jam (short for Theodore James, or something like that), was walking toward me.

I knew T-Jam vaguely from English class. Mostly he sat in the back row and made wisecracks. We weren't exactly pals, but we weren't enemies, either.

"What's up?" I said.

"Your locker's that way?" he asked, nodding in the direction in which I'd been headed.

"Yeah."

"Come on."

As we walked, he said, "I couldn't believe

you in class on Friday. You knew that stuff cold, man."

"You mean, about *Julius Caesar*?"

"Right, right," he said. "That play. Like, who the kings were and who said what. And what all those words meant."

I smiled. "I guess."

"I look at that homework, and like, I'm lost." He sighed and looked off in the distance. "I try. But it's like another language, you know? I mean I can see how it's like poetry and beautiful and stuff, but I can't answer any of the questions. I don't have the right, you know, *feel* for it, I guess."

"Yeah, it's pretty hard." I stopped in front of my locker and opened it.

T-Jam leaned against the locker next to mine. "If I flunk this class, I'm dead. I don't want to do eighth all over again. I think I need to, like, have some tutoring. Doesn't need to be a genius like you, but somebody who can explain stuff. You know anybody?"

I looked at T-Jam. Over his shoulder, I could see King and his pals rounding the corner. King's face lit up like a Christmas tree when he saw me. He began whispering to Peter and laughing.

King once got into a fight with one of the Badd Boyz — and lost. Ever since that he'd

13

been bad-mouthing them, calling them grease monkeys and piston heads. Different from the names he called *me*, but equally as clever.

You know what? I made a decision right there. My so-called friends on the track team were no better or worse than the Badd Boyz. At least T-Jam treated me like a human.

I opened my notebook and pulled out my English assignment. "Take a look at this," I said to T-Jam. "We can talk about it tomorrow, okay?"

For the first time ever, I saw him break a smile. "Thanks, man," he said. "What a dude."

He took the homework, clapped me on the shoulder, and walked back toward his friends.

King and the others moved away to let him pass. Their jaws were practically scraping the ground.

CHAPTER 2

"*Dreeeeeams of yoooou!*" Claudia Kishi wailed, holding a half-eaten Milky Way bar as if it were a microphone.

She sounded terrible. (Don't get me wrong. I like Claudia, but the truth is the truth.) Also a piece of chocolate was stuck on her front tooth, which made it look as if it were missing.

I began baying the way a dog does when a fire alarm goes off.

Mary Anne elbowed me.

"*Night and da-ay, day and ni-ight . . .*" Now Stacey McGill and Dawn Schafer had joined in.

Where was I? A Nicky Cash Fan Club convention? A voice therapy class for the musically challenged?

No. I was at the Monday meeting of the Baby-sitters Club, in Claudia Kishi's bedroom. Coach Leavitt had canceled our track team practice, so I had decided to attend the meeting. That afternoon, all nine members were present. Which meant eight Nicky Cash fans versus me.

"AW-ROOOOOO!" I repeated, which made the girls sing even louder.

A knock sounded at the door to the bedroom. Claudia's sister, Janine, peered in with a look of disgust. "What on *earth* are you doing?"

Everyone in the room dissolved into giggles. Janine just shook her head and left.

Claudia says her sister is an alien. Whenever Janine listens to music, it's classical. Her idea of funky clothing is a T-shirt with a picture of Mozart on it. Claudia thinks her sister's taste is a little weird. That Monday, I would definitely disagree.

Dawn Schafer sighed. "I heard Sabrina Bouvier got a ticket to the concert through her mom's company."

Groans all around.

"Come on, you guys," Kristy said, shaking her head. "I think we'll survive."

Finally. The Voice of Sanity.

Before anyone could say another word, Kristy switched to her Official voice: "Okay, this meeting will come to order!"

Wow. I absolutely did not see her look at Claudia's clock. She *must* have, but I could swear she hadn't. It had just clicked to five-thirty, the official starting time for BSC meetings. I think Kristy could be marooned on a South Sea island without a watch, and she'd still know when it was exactly five-thirty on a Monday, Wednesday, or Friday. And she'd probably cry out "Order!" to the seagulls.

Kristy, as you might guess, is the BSC president. She's also the one who thought up the idea for the club. And it's a great idea. It's so simple (and so *good*) you can't imagine why no one ever thought of it before.

Here's how it works. From five-thirty to six o'clock the BSC takes phone calls from parents who need sitters. Since there are seven regular members (and two of us associates), someone is always available to take the job.

Parents think the club is the best thing since the invention of the wheel. One phone call, one guaranteed sitter. And this is a nice arrangement for the regular club members, because they can count on steady work.

My prediction about Kristy: someday she's going to run a company. Or the country. You can tell by the way she set up the BSC — with officers, bookkeeping, and even advertising (mostly putting fliers in public places around town).

Kristy's constantly dreaming up new ideas for the club. Her mind never stops. Two of her original ideas (which we still use) are the

BSC record book and the BSC notebook. I'll get around to the record book later. The *notebook* is like a journal. In it, we write about our jobs — new information about our charges, helpful hints, funny stories, whatever. Sometimes this is a pain, but it's really helpful to everybody. Some of Kristy's ideas sound dumb: she suggested taking little old boxes crammed with secondhand toys and games ("Kid-Kits") to our sitting jobs. But guess what? Kids *love* them.

What's Kristy like?

Loud. No, seriously, she's very take-charge and energetic. She looks a little like Mary Anne, with brown hair and dark eyes, but Kristy's shorter. She's also the best athlete in the BSC, and in my opinion, the one who wears the most comfortable clothes — jeans, T-shirts, sweats, sneakers. She doesn't care about "fashion," but she looks fine.

Oh. Mary Anne and Kristy are best friends. Talk about opposites attracting.

Kristy has had a wild and complicated life. She grew up in a house across the street from Claudia's, but her dad split when she was six. And I mean *split*, just walked out on his wife and four kids. (Kristy has two older brothers, and a younger brother who was a newborn when her dad left.) Mrs. Thomas managed to raise the kids by herself — with Kristy's help,

I'm sure. In fact, Kristy invented the BSC after seeing how hard it was for her mom to line up a sitter. Anyway, when Kristy was twelve Mrs. Thomas met and married a guy named Watson Brewer. He happened to be a millionaire, and he happened to live in a mansion on the other side of town. So the Thomases moved in with him. It's so far away, Kristy has to be driven to meetings. (No, not in a chauffered limousine. Her brother Charlie drives her in his old jalopy.)

Kristy's new family is huge. Watson has two kids (Andrew and Karen) from a previous marriage who live there on alternate weekends. Plus he and Mrs. Thomas (now Mrs. Brewer) adopted a Vietnamese girl, Emily Michelle. To help take care of her, Kristy's grandmother moved in. And there's also a whole zoo of pets.

And that's not the only stepfamily in the BSC. Mary Anne has one, too. And she has also had an unusual life. Her mom died when she was little. Her dad, Richard, was totally broken up about it. He sent Mary Anne to live with her grandparents while he tried to cope with the loss. When he took her back, he became super-protective. Up until seventh grade Mary Anne had to wear little-girl dresses, keep her hair in pigtails, and follow all these other strict rules. Now, don't get the wrong impression. Richard's a nice guy, and he meant well. But he's pretty old-fashioned to begin with, and I think he was worried about being a "perfect parent" (whatever that is).

Well, he's changed a lot since then, mostly because he fell in love — with Dawn Schafer's divorced mother! They got married, and Mary Anne got a new family. More about that later.

Mary Anne has the hardest job in the BSC. (And I *don't* mean being my girlfriend.) She's the secretary, which is really the backbone of the club, if you ask me. She's in charge of the official record book. That means she keeps a calendar of all sitting jobs; an up-to-date client list with addresses, phone numbers, and the rate each one pays; and a description of the special likes and dislikes of our charges. She has to know all the club members' schedules — doctors' appointments, dance classes, after-school activities. And she also manages to spread the jobs around so everyone gets a pretty equal number. (She doesn't *have* to do that, she just *does* it.) Did I mention that Mary Anne has a brilliant mind for organizing? Now you know.

Rrrrinnngg!

"Hewwo . . . *hrrrmph* . . . hello, Baby-sitters Club!" Claudia must have had the last glop of Milky Way in her mouth when she picked up the phone. I could tell she was on the verge of cracking up. "Hi, Mrs. Arnold. . . . This Thursday? I'll check. . . ."

She put her hand over the receiver and looked at Mary Anne. (Mrs. Arnold is a regular customer. She has twin daughters, Marilyn and Carolyn.)

"*Hewwo?*" Kristy whispered.

"Stop!" Claudia hissed, barely holding in her laughter.

"Claud, you're available," Mary Anne said.

"Go for it, Elmer," I piped up.

"Okay," Claudia squeaked into the receiver. "I'll see you Thursday at four-thirty. . . . 'Bye." She hung up.

The room exploded. Claudia's face had turned deep red. "Oh, my lord, she must think I'm a pig," she moaned.

"Hi, Mawiwyn and Cawowyn, you scwewy twins," I said, in a brilliant imitation of Elmer Fudd. "Wanna pway? Huh-huh-huh-huh. . . ."

Everyone laughed again. Claudia threw her candy wrapper at me.

Claudia, by the way, is a junk-food maniac. Her parents are not, which presents a problem. That's why Claud keeps candy bars and bags of chips and pretzels hidden all over her room. (Along with Nancy Drew books, which her parents also forbid, because they're not "literature.")

No, Claudia is not fat and pimply. There's another stereotype. She is, like, drop-dead gorgeous — thin as a model, with long, jet-black hair. She has almond-shaped eyes (she's Japanese-American) and perfect skin. Her body must have a secret way of turning sugar into vegetable protein or something.

Or maybe she just burns off calories with her artwork. She paints, draws, sculpts, and makes jewelry. You should see her stuff. She's going to be a pro someday.

Claud is our vice-president. Her room is club headquarters because she's the only BSC member with a private phone line. Her main duty is stuffing everyone's faces. She also ends up answering the phone when clients call during non-meeting hours.

Here's another thing you should know about Claudia. She can make weird clothes look cool. Once she went to school with a rattle in her hair, like a barrette. Another time she wore bell-bottomed pants exactly like ones I've seen in these embarrassing old photos of my parents in college. Only on Claudia, they looked . . . right. I don't know what it is about her.

If there were ever a BSC fashion contest, though, Claudia would face stiff competition from Stacey McGill. Stacey dresses in the most amazing clothes. She's from New York City, and you can sort of tell. She looks sophisticated and hip. And talk about gorgeous. Stacey has long blonde hair and a toothpaste-ad smile.

Okay, before I go on, let me just say one thing. I am only *reporting* about these girls so you know what they look like. If I compliment them, it's merely an observation. Don't get the wrong idea.

End of message.

Back to Stacey. She's the treasurer. On Mondays she collects dues (which everyone has to pay, except for us associate members). Needless to say, hers is the least popular job. The money from the treasury is spent helping Claudia with her phone bill, paying Charlie for gas money, and buying new things for Kid-Kits.

Stace is about the last person you'd expect to be at a meeting of chocoholics. She has diabetes, which means her body goes out of whack if she has takes in too much sugar. She has to inject herself with insulin daily, or else she could get very sick.

Don't worry, though. She can still wolf down chips and pretzels.

Stacey and her parents first moved to Stoneybrook when she was in seventh grade. Then they moved back to New York because of her dad's job. But things didn't work out for Mr. and Mrs. McGill. They got divorced, and Stacey and her mom decided to move back here again. Fortunately her dad still lives in the Big Apple, so she sees him pretty often.

Dawn Schafer doesn't have it quite so good. Both her dad and her younger brother live clear across the country in California. *But* she has a great stepsister!

I told you I'd explain that situation, so here goes. Now, you know Mr. Spier is, well, not the coolest guy in the world. Okay, the truth: he's *stuffy*. Dawn's mom, Sharon, on the other hand, is wild. She's pretty and acts young and has this crazy habit of leaving things in weird places. One time I found her left slipper in the dishwasher.

Hey, don't ask me.

Anyway, you know who used to be boyfriend-and-girlfriend in high school? You guessed it. Richard and Sharon. And the memories must have stuck, because they got married and are living happily ever after. Mary Anne and her dad moved into the Schafers' farmhouse, which was built in 1795. It looks like a big old haunted house. Dawn is convinced it *is*. For one thing, a secret passageway leads from the barn to her bedroom. For another, there's an ancient legend about the ghost of an original owner who supposedly still walks the property.

24

(Maybe *he's* the one who put the slipper in the dishwasher.)

Dawn is another BSC member who doesn't eat junk food. No, she doesn't have diabetes. It's voluntary. She simply loves health foods. Tofu, sprouts, seeds, nuts — I think she fights the squirrels for acorns in the park. Just kidding. I guess I just come from a meat-and-potatoes kind of family. (Once my dad *did* buy some tofu at the supermarket, but that's because he thought it was cheese.)

I have to admit, Dawn looks awfully healthy. She's always tan and trim, and she has really long silky blonde hair. She's also concerned about the environment. Some kids tease her about it, but Dawn doesn't care. She stands up for what she believes in. I admire that.

Dawn's our alternate officer. She fills in for the others if they can't make meetings.

Mallory Pike and Jessica Ramsey are our two junior officers. They're eleven and in sixth grade (the rest of us are thirteen and in eighth). They're also best friends. They like to talk about books and complain that their parents treat them "like babies." Both are talented. Jessi's a great ballet dancer. She can do all these fancy leaps, twiddle her legs in the air (I don't know the real name for that, but it's very impressive), and balance on her toes.

They say dancers are the best athletes, better than football players, and I believe it. (Come to think of it, I'd like to see King in toe shoes.)

Jessi's the only African-American in the BSC. And since very few blacks live in Stoneybrook, her family did not have an easy time when they moved here. You wouldn't believe how much stupid prejudice they had to put up with. Fortunately things have improved a lot.

Even though they're the youngest BSC members, Jessi and Mal are both the oldest kids in their families. Jessi has an eight-year-old sister named Becca and a baby brother named John Philip Ramsey, Jr. (Squirt, for short). Mal has *seven* brothers and sisters.

Mal has thick, curly red hair and lots of freckles. She wears glasses and braces, neither of which look bad on her (the braces are clear), but she still feels self-conscious about them.

Now on to the associate members. You already know about me, so that leaves Shannon Kilbourne. She lives in Kristy's neighborhood, and she goes to a private school called Stoneybrook Day School. She's a real after-school extra-curricular type, so she can't make meetings too often. She has curly blonde hair and blue eyes, and for some reason she puts black outliner (or whatever you call that) around her eyes.

So that's the lineup. And they were all munching on candy like crazy (except for Stacey, who was eating chips, and Dawn, who was eating a bag of hay or something). They were involved in this heated, passionate argument.

"I saw his baby picture in a magazine," Claudia said. "The eyes were blue!"

"All babies' eyes are blue," Kristy replied.

"I heard you could make your eyeballs *white* with contact lenses if you wanted to," Stacey piped up.

"Those aren't lenses!" Claudia insisted. "I heard him say so on TV."

Dawn groaned. "You can't believe everything you hear on TV."

Guess who they were talking about. Not me, that's for sure.

I hope the BSC doesn't sound like a bunch of groupies — because they're not. I'd never seen them act like this before Nicky Cash came along. Oh, well. My mom is about the sanest person I know, and she told me she used to go to sleep with a picture of Paul McCartney under her pillow in the 1960s. I guess there are just some performers who bring out the strangeness in people.

You know, to tell you the truth, I didn't feel jealous of Nicky Cash at all. Looking at Mary Anne, I had this urge to surprise her with tickets to the concert. Just to see her expression.

If only I had a huge fortune, and a relative who worked at the stadium.

I guess she'd just have to settle for a custom-reserved copy of the CD. And a date with me.

Life is full of compromises, isn't it?

3

"Heyyy, Logan, planning any more *field trips?*"

It was Tuesday morning, time for the Clarence King Comedy Show. Lucky me. I was getting my own private performance, right in front of my locker. His laugh track was courtesy of Bob Stillman and Peter Hayes.

I could tell the Saturday meet wasn't fading from their minds.

"I was thinking of the Museum of Natural History," I replied, "but they might mistake you for one of the exhibits."

"Who-o-o-oa!" said Bob.

(Not bad, huh? I tell you, if *you* listened to King long enough, you'd come up with instant one-liners, too.)

"Come on, can't you take a joke?" King said. "Lighten up, dude. I don't know, maybe you've been hanging around with the girls too much."

Enough was enough. I whirled around to face him eye-to-eye. "What's that supposed to mean?"

"Oops! I'm not supposed to talk about that. Sorry!" With that dumb smirk, he pretended to back off. "No offense, Bruno. See you next *fall*!"

Peter and Bob burst out laughing.

For a moment I saw red. My stomach clenched. I wanted to jump on King's back. I wanted to tear him apart. Make him scream for forgiveness.

But I didn't do a thing. I don't exactly know why. I guess I didn't want to get suspended for fighting. Or maybe I just didn't feel like sinking to King's level.

That was when I heard T-Jam's voice. "Yo, Bruno. What's up?"

"Huh?" I turned toward him. A couple of other Badd Boyz were with him, looking tough as usual.

T-Jam gave me a puzzled look. "You all right?"

"Uh . . . yeah," I said.

He came close. Looking both ways, he took my English assignment out of his inner jacket pocket as if he were an international spy. "Thanks, man. You saved me. Seriously, I learned more from this than, like, a whole year of English class."

"No problem," I replied. (The paper was kind of wrinkled, which I wasn't too happy about.)

"No, really, I appreciate it," T-Jam said. "You're the only smart kid in this whole dump who's *cool*, you know what I mean? You ever need a favor. . . ."

I smiled. "Okay, T-Jam. Thanks, buddy."

"Any time. I mean it."

T-Jam and his friends began walking away. As I turned toward my homeroom, I noticed King's friends staring at me.

"Lo-*gannnn*," Bob said with a raised eyebrow. "Hanging with the Badd Boyz. . . ."

"So *that's* what happened Saturday!" King said. "Logan must have had too much axle grease on his sneakers."

"Yo! You got something to say?"

It was T-Jam. He and the two other Badd Boyz were heading toward King. Their eyes were blazing.

Before King could open his mouth, T-Jam was inches away from him. "I *said*, you got something to say, leather breath? Or did you just swallow a football? Huh?"

Leather breath? It was dumb. It made no sense. But it was funny.

I had never seen King look so defensive.

"Back off, man," he said. "Just joking with a friend."

"Yeah, who?"

King looked confused.

"I said, *who*? Not Logan?"

"Yeah," King said.

"Uh-uh, fumble face. Because I know a guy like Logan would never be friends with an ape like you. He could have you as a *pet* — only you probably haven't had your shots."

Whoa! Did he practice this stuff?

I couldn't believe King's reaction. I mean, he's at least two inches taller than T-Jam and about fifteen pounds heavier. But he just backed away like a puppy. "Knock it off, T-Jam. I wouldn't want to hurt you."

T-Jam laughed. "Try me, dude. Just try me."

With that, King was gone.

T-Jam turned to me as if nothing had happened. "See you at lunch?" he said. "We'll be sitting near the door — for awhile, at least."

"Um, yeah, well, I guess. . . ."

"No sweat. If you do, cool. If not, not. See you." With that, T-Jam and his friends left.

I felt like laughing all the way to homeroom. Too bad T-Jam wasn't on the track team. We could use a good pole vaulter. Hmmm. . . .

* * *

I usually sit with Mary Anne at lunch. On that day, though, she was meeting with some classmates to review for a math test. And for some strange reason, I didn't feel like sitting with King and my track teammates.

Now, until that day, I wouldn't have dreamed of eating lunch with the Badd Boyz. But I was still thinking about T-Jam's performance that morning. And it was still making me laugh.

I looked around. There they were, huddled in the back, a sea of black leather. T-Jam saw me and waved me over.

Aw, why not? I thought.

I didn't have to *be* a "Badd Boy." Lunch was lunch.

I walked to their table. " 'Tsup?" I asked.

"Nothing much," T-Jam said. "You know these guys? Skin, Ice Box, Butcher Boy, Jackhammer, G-Man . . ."

It sounded like a lineup of comic book heroes. I kept waiting for him to introduce *one* of them as "Charles" or "Percy," but no such luck.

"You guys eat yet?" I asked.

A couple of them smirked. "Nah," said the one called Ice Box, "we're dining el frisco."

"What's that?" I asked.

"It means outside," T-Jam said. "And it's el *fresco.*"

(It's not. It's *al fresco*. I looked it up later on.)

"Well — " (I tried not to look too uncool saying this, but our school does have rules.) "We can't really do that."

"Yeah? Want to see?" He looked over at Mr. Zizmore, a teacher who was standing in a corner. Mr. Z. was deep in conversation with Stacey McGill about something. "Come on."

T-Jam opened the rear door, and the Badd Boyz walked outside. Just like that.

Me? I followed them. I felt weird, but I was curious. And it wasn't such a big deal, really. I mean, it wasn't the kind of thing you could get suspended for.

We walked around a corner of the school and sat against the brick wall, facing the parking lot.

"Butt?" T-Jam asked.

He was holding out a cigarette. "Uh, no," I said.

"Cool. You got to keep your wind up for sports, am I right?"

"Right."

He and one of the others lit up. I just sat there, amazed that I was doing this.

It felt *great*! I don't know why, it just did.

I opened my bag lunch — and immediately realized no one else had one. Slowly I unwrapped my bologna sandwich. I felt very self-conscious.

"Save your appetite," Jackhammer said.

"For what?" I asked.

He shrugged. "Something. We don't know yet."

I was pondering that statement when a car came roaring into the parking lot.

Car? This thing was more like a sculpture on wheels. It was painted a star-speckled blue, and those shining silver pipes stuck out all over. Its wheels were huge, which made the rest of the car look sort of silly. As if it had shrunk in the car wash.

It screeched to a stop in front of us. Its windows were pitch-black, but the one on the driver's side was rolled down. A guy with beard stubble and a pair of mirrored sunglasses looked out. He seemed bored to see everybody. "Little bros," was all he said.

"Yo," T-Jam answered.

After this emotional greeting, a guy climbed out of the passenger side with two pizza boxes. He was wearing a Badd Boyz jacket.

"All riiiiiight!" G-Man said.

Everybody flipped into a good mood. The pizzas were set down and opened up. There was plenty for everyone.

"Who's the dude?" the driver asked.

"Name's Bruno," T-Jam said. "He's a genius, but he's, like, fully cool."

"Yeah? Hey, crispy, man," the older guy said, finally lightening up. "I'm Damon, but everybody calls me D. This is Remo."

I shook their hands. "Uh, thanks for the pizza."

"Yeah. Remo's uncle has a pizza shop at the strip mall. So sometimes we feed our little bros."

D took off his jacket. Immediately the others did too. Both D and Remo were wearing T-shirts with cigarette packs rolled up in the sleeves.

We dug into the pizzas. I took a slice of pepperoni and it was fantastic.

But I couldn't help wondering what these guys were doing here. It was the middle of the day. Weren't they supposed to be in school? Kids aren't allowed to just drive away from the high school whenever they feel like it.

Are they?

I was going to ask about it, but I didn't. What if they were dropouts? What if they didn't want to talk about it?

I figured I'd just eat my pizza and shut up.

D and Remo ended up asking *me* a few questions — about sports, about my family, about my "genius" reputation. I managed to get off a few jokes. Then, after we had finished eating, they got back in the car, said good-bye, and left.

"Pretty good 'za, huh?" T-Jam said.

Jackhammer grinned. "Was I right about your appetite?"

"Yep," I said.

We turned and went back inside, just before the bell rang for the end of the period. No one said a word to us.

Painless. And kind of fun. I hadn't had to listen to King's sick humor. And to be honest, it was kind of a nice change from listening to girl-talk at the BSC table.

Although Stacey and Dawn *were* giving me the strangest looks as they walked toward the door.

I just smiled and waved.

They must have seen me go outside. Oh, well, I didn't really care. It wasn't a big deal at all.

Well, word travels fast. Mary Anne was upset as we walked home from school that afternoon.

"They *asked* me to eat with them, that's all," I explained. "One of them is in my English class. He stuck up for me against King."

"But Logan, they are so . . . gross," Mary Anne said. "You don't even *look* like those guys."

I laughed and put my arm around her. "Not yet. I was thinking of growing my hair, buying a leather jacket, and . . . maybe stealing a Nicky Cash CD."

"Stop!" Mary Anne said, a sly smile growing on her face. "Except *maybe* for that last part . . ."

I pretended to be shocked. "Mary *Anne!*"

"Kidding!" she said. "Just kidding!"

CHAPTER 4

Thrusday

One bad thing about siting for twines. If its an off day, its twise as off. And OFF is a nice word to discribe this afternoon. It was imposable to talk to Caralyn and maralyn. I almost gave up on them. I think if I'd ben their another oh, seven or eigth hours I migth have made some head way....

Claudia has a lot going for her, but her spelling stinks. I guess you noticed that. (Whatever you do, don't tell her I said that, or she might bean me with a Twinkie.)

She is fantastic with kids, though. They love her sense of humor. She also thinks up great art projects for them.

When the Arnold twins came home from school, Claudia was waiting for them with a huge sketchpad. (Mr. and Mrs. Arnold were both working till dinnertime.)

"Hi!" Claudia called out as Marilyn and Carolyn ran through the back door.

"Where's Mom?" was Carolyn's reply.

"At a fundraiser," Claudia said. "Look what I brought."

The twins looked at the sketch pad blankly. "Is that for us?" Marilyn asked.

"Well, it's mine, but I thought we'd make weird creatures — you know, face of pig, body of fish, legs of bull. . . ."

"Uh-huh," Carolyn said. Her face looked gray and hollow. Claudia could swear she was about to cry.

"Are you okay?" Claudia asked.

"Yeah."

The girls took off their sweat shirts and went into the kitchen. Claudia followed them. "Did something happen at school?"

40

"No," Marilyn said.

"Okay. Well . . . are you guys hungry for a snack?" Claudia asked.

Carolyn and Marilyn shot each other a glance. Then they nodded.

"Cheese and crackers?"

"Uh-huh."

Claudia made a plate of saltines and American cheese. The minute she put it on the table, the twins gobbled up every last piece.

Then Claudia brought out a bunch of green grapes, and they devoured that, too.

"Whoa, you guys are *hungry*," Claudia said.

"Could you make me a cream-cheese-and-jelly sandwich, please?" Marilyn said, still munching. "On a bagel?"

"Me, too!" Carolyn added.

"Wait a minute," Claudia said. "You're going to eat dinner when your mom and dad come home."

"But we're starving!" Carolyn protested.

"Didn't you guys have enough for lunch?" Claudia asked.

Silence.

Marilyn looked at the floor. "We didn't have anything," she whispered.

Carolyn glared at her.

"Why not?" Claudia asked.

More silence.

"Did you lose your lunches?" Claudia tried.

"No."

"Did your parents forget to pack them?"

"No."

"Did a dinosaur follow you to school and sit on them?"

"No!" (Claud thought that would make them laugh, but they just sounded annoyed.)

Claudia folded her arms. "Are you two telling me the truth?"

Marilyn's bottom lip folded downward. "EJ *took* it."

"*Marilyn!*" Carolyn hissed.

"Who's EJ?" Claudia said.

"Nobody," Carolyn snapped.

Marilyn lowered her head again.

It was time to use a tried-and-true BSC strategy: Never try to force a reluctant kid. Just repeat what they say in a sympathetic way — and be patient.

"So, EJ took your lunch, Marilyn?" Claudia said gently. "That must have made you feel awful."

"It did!" Marilyn agreed.

"Me, too!" said Carolyn.

Claudia nodded. "What a mean thing to do."

"Yeah!" Marilyn said. "EJ is such a bully!"

Their faces were red now. Claudia felt sorry for them. Obviously they'd been humiliated by some elementary school tough guy.

I guess every grade has its own Clarence King.

"Did you tell your teacher?" Claudia asked.

Both Marilyn and Carolyn mumbled "No." Claudia decided not to bug them about it. She could see they felt embarrassed about telling what had happened.

"Well, no wonder you're starving," Claudia said. "You haven't had a bite since breakfast!"

She made them the sandwiches, even though she knew they might spoil their appetites for dinner. As the girls tore into the sandwiches, Claudia sat at the table and opened her sketchpad to a blank page. "You know," she said, "we can figure out ways to deal with bullies. Can you think of some?"

Marilyn and Carolyn sat there, thinking and chewing. "Um, go a different way to school," said Carolyn.

"Good," replied Claudia. "I'll write it down, so you can have a reminder."

"Buy lunch at school," Marilyn suggested.

Claudia scribbled that down, too.

"But then EJ might steal your money," Carolyn said.

"Oh. Then we can put, like, slime on our money."

Carolyn rolled her eyes. "Yeah, that would be great for our hands and pockets."

"What about just ignoring him?" Claudia

said. "Or walking with a group of friends?"

"I know!" Carolyn cried, her mouth full of cream cheese, "we can pack liverwurst sandwiches. Then when EJ takes a bite — ewwww!"

Marilyn laughed. "Or put mud in the sandwich."

"Or caterpillars!"

"Or seaweed!"

(It was a good thing Dawn wasn't sitting. She would not have laughed at that last idea.)

As for Claudia, I think she gave up on the list. She was happy the twins were in a good mood. After they ate, they went into the den and yakked away. They seemed to want to be alone, so Claud stayed in the kitchen and did some sketching of her own. But she caught a few snatches of conversation about the bully — plans for bringing bombs to school, setting bear traps, ambushing from the trees, dressing up as ghosts, and dumping EJ into the sewer.

By the time Mrs. Arnold came home, Marilyn and Carolyn were conquering the world. Claudia left before the topic of dinner had a chance to come up.

You know what bothered Claudia most about that afternoon? She couldn't figure out why it was so hard for the twins to talk to *her* about EJ. It wasn't as if Claudia were some grown-up.

She had a feeling there was more to the story.

"I'm home!" she yelled as she walked into her house.

"Hi, home," Janine called from the top of the stairs. "Stacey called. She said to call back right away."

Claudia ran upstairs to her room and tapped out Stacey's number.

"Hello?" Stacey said on the other line.

"Hi, it's me," Claudia said. "What happened?"

"Claudia, hi! Did you leave any of your jewelry in your locker?"

"Um . . . just those funky earrings I made with feathers and buttons. Why?"

"Because Erica Blumberg left a necklace in hers — and it was stolen."

"Stolen? In school? Come on, Stacey, you know Erica. She probably dropped it somewhere."

"She swears it was there, Claudia. And they messed up her locker, too. The same thing happened to a few other kids, she says."

"I didn't know so many girls left jewelry in their lockers."

"Not just jewelry, Claudia. And not just in lockers, either. Gordon Brown's jacket was stolen in the cafeteria, *two* of Janet Gates's CDs were taken in the library, and Trevor Sandbourne knows someone whose sunglasses were taken in the bathroom."

"That's terrible," Claudia said. "I guess we'll have to be careful."

"Yeah."

They fell silent. Finally Stacey sighed and said, "How were the twins?"

"Don't ask," Claudia replied. "Some bully took their lunch, and they're both planning to, like, dynamite him."

"Mm-hm. There's a lot of bad karma going around."

"Bad caramel?"

"*Bad karma.* Dawn says that, you know, when things get creepy."

"Yeah," Claudia said. "I guess she's right."

"Oh, well, I have to go. See you tomorrow."

" 'Bye."

Claudia hung up, feeling depressed. But Stacey had planted a thought in her mind. She reached into her closet, rummaged around in a shoe box, and found a bag of caramels.

She felt much, much better.

Leave it to Claudia.

CHAPTER 5

My life was changing. Just a little, but for the better. For one thing, I had learned something important about dealing with King.

All this time I'd been trying to rise above him and his insults. I'd thought that if I did well in sports and didn't sink to his level, everything would be all right. Well, I'd been wrong. Now I was trying a new plan.

"Hey, Lois, you skipping the Baby-sitters Club today?" was the way King greeted me at track practice that Friday afternoon. "What's the matter, the girls are hogging all the Ken dolls?"

I stared at him through half-squinted eyes. I tried not to show any expression on my face. "Are you saying something to me?" I asked.

King just snickered and said, "You heard me."

I stood my ground. "Guess again."

I couldn't believe it. King's smile was fading. He sneered and jogged off to run a lap.

Not bad, huh? I didn't have to *be* a gang member to sound like one.

Something else. I was *great* in practice that day. I ran the fastest hundred-yard dash in my life, and broke my record for the high jump. I even tried the pole vault (which isn't my event) and beat the regular guy.

"Looking good, Bruno," Coach Leavitt called out at one point, and he doesn't give compliments easily.

Now, don't get the wrong impression. I'm not saying that the Badd Boyz had magically transformed my life. I mean, let's face it, Mary Anne was right. I was a much different kind of person than they were. I would never dress like they did, or smoke, or be so antisocial.

But here's what I liked about them:

1. They didn't care what people thought of them.

2. They weren't afraid of anybody or anything.

3. They were loyal to their friends.

When you looked under the surface, they were an okay bunch of guys. I kind of admired their independence.

And you know what else? I feel funny admitting this, but being around them was *ex-*

citing. Me, Mr. Nice Guy-Athlete. Mr. L. L. Bean Wardrobe.

Anyway, I found out T-Jam was going to the strip mall on Atlantic Avenue that Saturday. (The mall is one of those old-fashioned outdoor ones, with an L-shaped line of stores.) I wanted to buy Mary Anne that CD, so I agreed to meet him there.

I waited in front of Sound Ideas for a few minutes. Then I saw T-Jam come out of a sporting goods store with Ice Box and Butcher Boy.

What a picture. T-Jam is fair-haired and lean, Ice Box is dark and built like a linebacker, and Butcher Boy's about five feet one and looks like he eats ice cream for every meal.

I walked over to them. " 'Tsup?"

"*Nada*, man," T-Jam said.

"Check these out." Ice Box pulled a pair of black bicycle gloves out of his inner jacket pocket — the kind with the fingers cut off at the top. He put them on and said, "Like them?"

"Cool," I replied. (Well, they were.)

Ice Box gave T-Jam a grin, then glanced back toward the store.

"Stuff them, man," T-Jam muttered.

Ice Box put the gloves back in his pocket.

Butcher Boy looked over my shoulder toward the cineplex. "Yo, one of the movies is letting out. Want to go to *Nightmare High*? It's playing."

"Nah," I said. "I didn't bring enough money for — "

"You don't need it," Butcher Boy said.

"Huh?"

"See that rear exit that's open? If you hang out nearby while the people come out, you can duck inside without paying," T-Jam explained. "No sweat."

"Well, I have to get back home pretty soon," I said, "and I'm supposed to get this CD for my girlfriend."

"From your buddy at Sound Ideas?" T-Jam asked.

"My buddy?" I said.

"Yeah, the guy who owns the place," T-Jam replied. "I saw you talking to him last week in the store."

"You were there?"

"Yeah. But you didn't see me, or you didn't know who I was."

I felt a little guilty. I could vaguely remember seeing T-Jam at the store. "Well, yeah. My dad's a friend of his."

"So you get a deal, huh?" Ice Box said.

"Sometimes," I answered. "But I don't *ask* for it or anything — "

"Sure, sure," T-Jam said. "That would be

rude, like something Ice would do."

"*Squank*," Ice Box said, and gave T-Jam a joking punch.

We walked to Sound Ideas. As we went in, Bob Shull looked up from the counter. He was running a credit card check on a customer. "Hi, Logan," he said. "Be with you in a minute, okay?"

"Okay," I replied.

T-Jam and I looked at a display of Nicky Cash CDs and tapes. There was a full-color, life-sized cardboard likeness of him, shirtless and smirking. "His name is, like, Archibald Fender or something," T-Jam said.

"Reginald Fenster," I corrected.

We both started laughing. Somehow the idea of this sweating macho heartthrob as a *Reginald* seemed hilarious.

Out of the corner of my eye, I could see Ice Box and Butcher Boy in the Heavy Metal section.

"Well, what can I do for you?"

T-Jam and I turned to see Bob approaching. He's a tall, burly guy with blond hair and an open, friendly face.

"I'm going to get one of these," I said, gesturing toward Nicky Cash.

(Nicky's expression didn't change a bit. The ingrate.)

Bob smiled and rolled his eyes. "You and a

million girls. I think you're the first guy who's asked."

Now, if *King* had been there, I would have heard about that remark for a whole week. But T-Jam just said, "It's for his girlfriend."

Bob nodded and took a CD off the top. "It's a good thing you came now. These'll sell out by Wednesday, guaranteed. I had to order another shipment — and the earliest they'll deliver is next Saturday."

"Whoa," T-Jam said. "And probably not till after you close, right?"

"Well, they said ten A.M., and they're usually pretty good for it," Bob replied. "By then, I'll have a line out the door. Come on, I'll ring you up." He began walking to the register.

T-Jam eyed his friends, who were behind us and to the right. Butcher Boy looked up quickly, then back down again.

"I see you're having a sale on jazz CDs," T-Jam said suddenly.

The jazz shelf was to our left. Bob turned and walked to it. "We sure are," he replied. "Who do you like?"

"Um . . . I like him." T-Jam pointed to a Miles Davis CD.

Bob smiled and took the CD off the shelf. "Miles, huh? You have good taste. Do you play?"

"Huh?" T-Jam said.

"The horn," Bob replied. "Like Miles."

"Oh . . . nah," T-Jam said. "But maybe I'll learn."

"Anything else?" Bob asked.

"Yeah . . . how about, um, that John Coltrane CD?"

As Bob reached for that one, T-Jam looked over his shoulder. Ice Box and Butcher Boy were walking out of the store.

Bob led T-Jam and me to the counter. I paid for my CD, and then Bob rang up T-Jam's disks. "That'll be twenty-seven ninety-seven."

T-Jam reached into his pockets. He pulled out a couple of singles and a pack of gum. "Oh, no!" he exclaimed. " I was supposed to bring my old man's credit card. I must have forgotten it!"

"Hey, it happens all the time," Bob said. "You want me to hold the CDs for a week or so?"

"Thanks," T-Jam said. "Sorry, man."

"No problem. Take care, guys. Say hi to your dad, Logan."

"Okay. 'Bye."

T-Jam and I walked out of the store. Ice Box was already in the center of the mall, sitting on the ledge of a big water fountain.

"Where's Butch?" T-Jam asked.

"Shopping," Ice Box said with a funny grin.

I reached into my pocket. It was time to call

my parents for a ride home. "I'll be at the pay phone," I said.

"You want a lift?" T-Jam offered. "D's coming in a couple minutes."

"Sure," I said.

A moment later, I saw Butcher Boy come out of an electronics store. He was walking very fast. "Let's book," he said.

T-Jam and Ice Box sprang up. We all jogged through the parking lot.

Okay, let me say this right out. I am no dope. I could tell *something* was going on. I mean, running away from the mall after your friend leaves a gadget store? Hiding bicycle gloves? And what about Sound Ideas? I wasn't convinced T-Jam was a jazz fan — or that he even knew who Miles Davis and John Coltrane were. Not to mention the stuff about forgetting his dad's card. It seemed as though T-Jam was trying to distract Bob for some reason.

Were they stealing things? They hadn't unzipped their leather jackets the whole time we'd been indoors. Possibly they were hiding stuff, but the jackets were so bulky it was hard to tell.

And I wasn't about to ask, "Excuse me, do you have shoplifted goods in your pockets?"

Besides, maybe I was wrong. To these guys,

acting shady was second nature. Cool. Part of the image.

As we slowed to a walk, my new pals eyed the cars in the lot. I got a running commentary.

"Whoa, a Lamborghini. . . ."

"Look at the alarm system in that Porsche."

"That Ferrari would make me happy."

T-Jam stopped in front of a pretty average-looking car. He glanced around, then grabbed the passenger-door handle.

The door swung open. T-Jam reached inside and took a pair of sunglasses from the dashboard. When he slammed the door shut, he and the other two began running. "Come on, Logan!" T-Jam shouted.

I followed them to the sidewalk. They were laughing. T-Jam put on the glasses and looked around. "Decent shades," he remarked.

I had to say something. "Why did you do that?" I asked.

"Hey," T-Jam said with a shrug. "They shouldn't have left their door open. I could have taken a lot more than this cheap thing. Next time they'll remember, right?"

"Come on," I said, "that's no excuse. Those glasses don't belong to you."

T-Jam took them off and tapped them in his hands. "You know, man, you're right. I mean, I just saw them there and, like, the temptation got to me, you know?" He began walking back to the car.

Ice Box and Butcher Boy looked flabbergasted. "You're going to put them *back*?" Ice Box said.

"What does it look like, Einstein?" T-Jam snapped. He shook his head and said, "Come on, Bruno. These guys have no manners, you know what I mean?"

We walked all the way to the car. T-Jam did return the glasses. He even locked the door before he closed it.

As we headed back toward the guys, T-Jam gave me a lopsided smile. "You're quality, Bruno. I mean that. Real quality."

CHAPTER 6

"What's that supposed to mean?" Mary Anne asked. " 'You're quality'? It sounds like he's talking about a . . . a kitchen appliance or something."

It takes a lot for Mary Anne to get worked up. I guess my hanging out with the Badd Boyz counted as "a lot."

It was Monday, after school. I was in my track uniform, standing by the field and waiting for practice to start officially. That morning, D had given me a ride to school with T-Jam, and I'd eaten lunch with the Badd Boyz. I hadn't talked to Mary Anne since Saturday.

Big Mistake Number One.

So what did I bring up first? My adventure in the mall — minus some details, of course, like my suspicions about the shoplifting.

Big Mistake Number Two.

"I didn't mean for you to get upset," I

said. "I just thought it was kind of a funny story."

Mary Anne's voice softened. "Oh, Logan, I don't mean to sound upset. It's just that . . . well, it's so hard to believe you actually like those guys."

"Mary Anne, they're not so bad," I said. "Really. People have the wrong impression."

"They cut school, they're always making snotty comments in the hallway, they smoke. Logan, do you think it's a good idea to come home to your brother smelling like cigarette smoke? With his allergies?"

"*I* don't smoke!"

"Not to mention all the stealing that's been going on. Who knows . . ." Her voice trailed off.

"What stealing?" I asked.

Mary Anne exhaled. "Some kids have had stuff taken out of their lockers. Stacey told me about it."

"Wow," I said. "That's terrible."

Phweeeeeet!

It was the familiar sound of Coach Leavitt's whistle. I had to go. "Oh!" I said. "I almost forgot, I have a surprise for you."

Mary Anne looked at me blankly for a second. Then her face lit up. "A Nicky Cash cassette!"

I cast my eyes downward sadly. "Well . . . uh, no."

I wish the Oscar committee had seen my performance. Mary Anne looked disappointed and embarrassed at the same time. "Well . . . that's okay," she said. "What is it?"

"It's a Nicky Cash *CD*," I replied. "That was why I went to the mall."

"*Really?*" Mary Anne jumped up and down, then threw her arms around me. "Oh, thanks, Logan, that's so sweet!"

Phweet-phweeoooo!

That was *not* Coach Leavitt's whistle. It had come from King, Peter Hayes, Bob Stillman, or Steve Randazzo. They were all standing at the edge of the field, grinning at Mary Anne and me.

"Smile for the camera!" Steve said, pretending to take a picture.

"Logan-Pogan, Pudding and Pie, kissed the girls and made them cry!" Peter sang.

King just made loud, sloppy kissing noises. Very classy.

Mary Anne's face turned red. "I better go," she whispered. " 'Bye . . . and thanks!"

"I'll call later," I whispered back.

As she walked away, King started prancing around in a stupid, exaggerated way that was supposed to look like a girl's walk.

I wanted to pound him. Fortunately, Coach Leavitt was standing right there, *not* looking happy.

"You're a barrel of laughs, King," he said sharply. "Let's see you imitate a long-distance runner. Ten laps. Now!"

"Aw, Coach . . ." King began to complain.

"In under twenty minutes." The coach took out his stopwatch and began timing.

In a flash, King was off.

And I was off the hook.

About halfway through practice, guess who showed up in the stands? Well, not actually *in* the stands, but leaning against them, with upturned collars and cigarettes dangling from their mouths.

No, not the memberes of the Baby-sitters Club (ha ha). It was T-Jam, this time with Skin. (His real name is Dennis Malek. The nickname comes from a pigmentation problem that causes white patches on his face. He doesn't seem to mind it. I guess there's a fine line between cruel and cool.)

Of course my teammates noticed them. But you know what? No one dared make a comment to me. I overheard King mutter, "Look, it's the Dead End Kids," but he said it to Steve.

In fact, all of my teammates seemed to steer

clear of me in the locker room. Even the guys I liked, such as Lew Greenberg. That was a little weird.

When I stepped into the hallway, T-Jam and Skin were waiting. " 'Tsup?" T-Jam said.

"What are you guys doing here?" I asked.

"I forgot something in my locker," T-Jam replied. "Only the janitor won't let me in the main part of the school. Maybe if I go with you . . ."

"No problem," I said. "Come on."

I waved to the custodian as we walked to the lockers. He just smiled and waved back. "It's really not fair," I said under my breath. "Why should he let me in and not you?"

"What are *you* worried about?" Skin asked.

T-Jam shot him a glance. "Some thanks, cheese face. Bruno is doing us a favor."

Even though I really didn't need to, I opened my locker and rummaged around inside. T-Jam went to his, which was halfway down the hall.

Skin disappeared around the corner.

After a while T-Jam began throwing things around loudly. "Now where is . . . man, I know I left it here."

"You lose something?" I asked.

"My English textbook. I always keep it on the top shelf, and — "

"Take it easy, man," I said. "We don't need

the book for homework. It's a creative-writing assignment, remember?"

"Oh, yeah, that's right. I forgot." He straightened out his locker and closed it. "Like I said, you are a genius. Let's get out of here. I need a soda or something."

He started walking back toward the doors.

"Wait, what about Skin?" I said.

"Skin? Oh, uh, I think he must have left already — "

"No, he went this way. I saw him." I began jogging down the hall.

"Bruno, where are you going?" T-Jam shouted.

"Hey, Skin!" I called out as reached the corner.

I stopped short. Skin was there, all right. Prying open someone's locker with a screwdriver. He looked up at me, then kept on prying.

"What's going on?" I said.

T-Jam ran up beside me. "Is this familiar or what?" he said. "Your lock stuck again?"

"Yeah, yeah," Skin mumbled.

The locker popped open. Skin looked inside, then grabbed a small cassette recorder from the top shelf. He stuffed it into his jacket pocket, then slammed the door shut.

Now, I was willing to give him the benefit

of the doubt. I didn't know this section of lockers too well, and some locks *have* stuck before.

But I had seen a girl's sweater hanging from one of the hooks inside.

"That's *your* locker?" I asked.

Skin glowered at me. "What's it to you?"

"That's not right, Skin," was the only thing I could think of saying.

"What are you going to do about it?"

T-Jam grabbed me by the arm and led me away. "Look, Bruno," he said in a hushed voice, "Skin is, well, not exactly playing with a full deck, if you smell my meaning."

"*What?*"

"I mean, he has this, like, klepto thing. His 'rents are sending him to a shrink, you know, but I guess it's not working yet. See, he doesn't think that what he's doing is wrong."

"That's no excuse, T-Jam. I mean, we're talking a *crime* here."

"Bruno, please, don't get carried away."

"*Carried away?*" I was starting to see red. All my suspicions just tumbled out. "Maybe I *should* get carried away. What about Saturday? The sunglasses from the car, the bicycle gloves, Butcher Boy and Ice Box at Sound Ideas — "

T-Jam looked stunned. "Hey, Bruno, just because I did a stupid thing in the parking lot, you don't have to accuse my friends of being thieves." He shook his head and narrowed his eyes at me. "Man, you're just like everybody else. I'm out of here."

With that, he turned and walked away.

My anger fizzled away like air from a balloon. "T-Jam, come on. I didn't mean to accuse anybody. But you can't just cover up for Skin. Think of the person who owns that recorder. It's not fair."

T-Jam turned around and sighed. "You got a point there. But hey, what can we do?"

"I don't know. What do you think?"

"We can't rat on Skin, right?"

I shrugged. "Well, it might be the best thing, in the long run."

T-Jam's glance turned cold. "Bruno, you're a good guy. I like you. But you got to realize something. If you do that to Skin, they're going to want to know what *you* were doing here."

I just stared at him. I felt my throat going dry.

"That's right," T-Jam said with a little nod. "Alone here, after hours, when nobody's around — very suspicious. They'll lump me and you and Skin together. You know, guilt by association. Like it or not, you're one of us now, Bruno."

CHAPTER 7

Wednesday

I don't know who this EJ is, but he's got all the kids scared out of their wits. Even mature, level-headed Charlotte. Today I sat for her, and she was so ~~strange~~. It was like, WHOA! Instant five-year-old!

I know we're supposed to let kids fight their own battles and all, but this is getting out of hand. I think somebody ought to step in and do something. If not us, then an adult...

I thought I had it bad. The kids in Stoney-brook Elementary School were being terrorized. No one had realized how widespread the EJ crisis was.

Stacey found out for herself when she babysat for Charlotte Johanssen.

I should mention that Char and Stace are really close. When Stacey first moved to Stoneybrook, Charlotte was an unbelievably smart seven-year-old who was also painfully shy and sad. Now she's an unbelievably smart eight-year-old who's friendly and outgoing. Stacey had a lot to do with the transformation. She really brought Char out of her shell. Now the two of them call each other "almost sisters."

Wednesday was one of those incredible early fall days — you could practically taste the fresh coolness of the air. Stacey was sure Char would want to play outdoors.

Stacey was wrong.

"No!" Charlotte said to the suggestion. "Becca's coming over, and we're going to play inside!"

"Well, sure, if you want," Stacey said. "But the weather is gorgeous — "

"I don't care!"

Stacey backed off. Charlotte seemed to be in her own world. She disappeared into the rec room, talking to herself. Stacey stayed in the kitchen and started her homework.

Three times Charlotte ran in and asked, "Did somebody knock?"

Three times Stacey said, "No." She figured Becca and Char must be involved in some weird game.

Finally the doorbell rang. Charlotte ran to the front of the house. She pushed back the window curtains and peered outside. "Whew!" she exclaimed. "It's only Becca."

Stacey opened the door. "Were you expecting someone else?"

Becca Ramsey rushed in, a grave expression on her face. "Hi, Stacey," she said.

"Hi, Becca! Nice day, huh?"

Becca didn't answer. She just looked at Char and said, "Is everything okay?"

Charlotte nodded. "So far, so good. Come on."

They ran into the rec room. Stacey sat down in the kitchen again, but she couldn't concentrate on her homework. She was too curious now.

In a minute, Charlotte rushed out of the rec room with a chair. She dashed into the front hallway. Becca followed her, holding a folded-up card table.

"Playing cards?" Stacey asked.

"No," Charlotte replied.

The girls disappeared into the rec room again. This time they came out with another chair and a big roll of tape. Once again, they ran into the hall. Stacey heard the familiar *rrrip* of tape being pulled off the roll.

After that they ran to the basement. Grunting, they carried up a heavy old gumball machine Mr. Johanssen has always kept down there. Stacey watched them prop it against the back door.

"Uh . . . may I ask what on *earth* you are doing?" Stacey asked.

"Putting stuff against the doors," Charlotte replied.

Duh.

"Uh-huh. Well . . . your dad's going to have a pretty tough time getting in, don't you think?"

"We'll let him in," Charlotte said.

"We just have to keep EJ out," Becca explained.

"Oh," Stacey said. "I see. Did EJ threaten to huff and puff and blow your house down?"

Becca giggled, but Charlotte shook her head solemnly. "No, just to come over and beat us up."

"So we have to EJ-proof the house," Becca said. "Come on, Char."

They raced around, finding things to jam

against the doors — a box of old toys, a small stepladder, even stuffed animals. Before long, they were giggling like crazy and bringing in things like Play-Doh cans and pillows.

Then they vanished into Charlotte's bedroom. For about fifteen minutes, all Stacey heard was an occasional stifled laugh.

Finally they came downstairs. Charlotte was wearing a big mustache and thick, angry eyebrows, courtesy of a black marker. Becca was wearing an orange clown wig and plastic fangs.

"Rrraaaaargh!" Becca said.

Stacey couldn't help laughing. "Charlotte Johanssen, what did you do to your face?"

"It's *washable*." Charlotte began running toward the basement door. "Come on, Becca. Let's make our potion."

"Potion?" Stacey said.

Becca took out her fangs. "Yeah. A magic potion that will make EJ shrink," she explained.

The two girls scampered downstairs.

It's just a game, Stacey told herself. But she was feeling a little creeped out. These kids were obsessed.

Obviously EJ was a pretty intimidating kid.

Stacey walked into the hallway and looked at the barricade. Thick, clear tape was plastered over the crack between the door and the doorjamb. Stuff was piled up, shoulder high. It looked like a rummage sale that never quite made it outside.

It also looked like something Charlotte would never do, and her parents would not approve of.

With a sigh, Stacey went down into the basement. Char and Becca were standing by the sink, pouring stuff into a measuring cup — water, detergent, potting soil, whatever they could get their hands on.

"Hey guys, that could be dangerous, you know," Stacey said.

Charlotte rolled her eyes. "It's *supposed* to be dangerous. It's *poison*."

"Um . . . don't you think this is going a bit far?" Stacey asked. "Is this EJ really so dangerous?"

Charlotte and Becca nodded.

Stacey sighed. "Look, maybe you should talk to a teacher about this. At least mention it to your parents — "

Charlotte's eyes grew wide. "You won't tell my parents, will you, Stacey? EJ will kill us if we tell."

"I'll leave it up to you," Stacey said. "But *I* think you should mention something. Maybe your parents can talk to EJ's parents."

Becca and Char stared at her as if she were crazy.

70

"Anyway, I can't let you play with this stuff," Stacey went on. "Please pour it out and come upstairs."

"Okay," Charlotte groaned.

Stacey trudged upstairs, followed soon after by Becca and Char. The girls returned to Char's room, and Stacey decided to give her English assignment a try. She reached into her purse and took out a small notebook, in which she'd written down the assignment.

That was when she noticed her wallet was gone.

She closed her eyes and thought. The last time she remembered seeing it was when she was in school. She had kept it in her bag constantly, ever since the locker thefts had started.

She tried to recall how much money was in it.

"Charlotte?" she called upstairs. "You didn't see my wallet lying around anywhere, did you?"

The girls appeared at the top of the stairs. "Is it missing?" Char asked.

"Uh-huh."

Charlotte and Becca gave each other a frightened look. "EJ probably took it," Char said.

Stacey tried to laugh. "Uh, I don't think so. I probably left it at home."

The girls went back into the room, and Stacey sank into her chair.

It had been stolen. She knew it. Not only couldn't she leave anything in her locker, now she had to watch her bag with an eagle eye.

Stacey could not believe this was happening in Stoneybrook. She felt as if she'd never left New York City.

CHAPTER 8

*H*onk! *Honnnnnnk!*

I barely noticed the car horn blaring outside. *Inside*, the Brunos were having a laid-back Saturday breakfast.

"Take your dinosaur off the table, Hunter, it's disgusting!" Kerry said.

"Rooooar! I'b godda eat you up!" Hunter said, imitating a tyrannosaurus with allergies.

"Your sister is right," my dad said. "We don't play with toys at the table."

Hunter climbed off his chair. But before he put his dinosaur away, he lunged it toward Kerry and said, "I'm an EJ-saurus, so watch out!"

"*Daaa-ad!*" Kerry screamed.

"Hunter! I want you in the time-out chair!" Dad bellowed.

"*Nooooooooo!*"

Remember Kerry's anti-school disease?

Well, you guessed it. The cause was none other than EJ.

Maybe T-Jam could recruit him for a junior chapter of the Badd Boyz. (The Badd Little Boyz?)

Honk! Honnnnnnk!

"What is going on out there?" my mom said.

I went to the living room and looked out the front window.

I saw D's car. I opened the front door and walked onto the porch.

"Little *bro!*" D called out.

I jumped down the steps and ran to the car. I could see Remo in the passenger seat, and T-Jam and Ice Box in the back. "Hey, what's up, guys?"

Remo got out and folded the front seat up. "Come on. We're going to the mall."

I laughed. "Well, wait a minute. This is kind of — "

"Don't you want to go?" D asked.

"Well . . . sure, but — "

"You need to ask your *parents*?" Remo said with a mocking grin.

"Yo, Remo, lighten up," T-Jam said from the backseat. "We're not middle-aged, like you dudes. I had to ask, too, all right?"

"Okay, okay," Remo grumbled.

"I'll be right back," I said.

I ran inside. Mom, Dad, and Kerry were still

eating eggs and bacon. I could hear Hunter making dinosaur noises from the living room.

"I'm going to the mall," I said, grabbing a windbreaker from the alcove behind the kitchen.

"Aren't you going to finish your breakfast?" my mom asked.

"I'm not hungry," I said.

"Say hi to Mary Anne," Kerry called out as I ran to the front door. I didn't bother to mention who I was really going with.

The last thing I heard as I closed the door behind me was Hunter's voice saying, "Is by tibe-out over *yet*?"

I trotted to the car and squeezed into the backseat with T-Jam and Ice Box. "Man, it's a good thing you ain't Butcher Boy," Ice remarked. "We'd be hurting back here."

D floored the accelerator. The car took off with a squeal of tires.

If my parents had looked out the front window, they would have been totally freaked. I'd vaguely mentioned T-Jam to them, but I never said anything about the car or the older guys.

Through the open window, the early autumn wind tossed my hair straight back and blew away some of the stale cigarette smell. I looked at T-Jam. His eyes were glimmering. "Weather, huh?" he said.

"Yeah." I smiled and looked straight ahead. D had turned onto Atlantic Avenue and was weaving through traffic. I could see people staring at the car as we passed.

This was *fun*. I had no idea why we were going to the mall or what we were going to do. All I knew was that T-Jam and Ice had gotten together with the older guys, and they had decided they wanted *me* along.

Go with the flow. That was what I told myself. Enjoy the ride.

We used the back entrance to the parking lot. As we drove in, we could see a truck backing up to a truck dock behind a store.

Bob Shull was standing near it, clipboard in hand.

"Hey, isn't that your friend?" Ice Box said.

"Yeah," I replied.

T-Jam looked at his watch. "Ten oh-six. I guess they came on time."

"Huh?"

"Remember what he said last week, about those Nicky Cash tapes?"

"Oh, right. He wasn't going to get a shipment till Saturday — "

"At ten A.M." T-Jam shrugged. "So I guess a lot of girls will be happy, huh?"

By this time, D had driven to the front of the parking lot. "You know that guy back there?" he said.

"Yeah," T-Jam replied.

D pulled the steering wheel to the right. All our bodies lurched to the left as he drove back the way we had come. He screeched to a stop just before the back wall of the stores and parked the car.

D and Remo got out of the car. "You guys go say hi to your friend if you want, then come hang with us."

I guessed that was the point of coming — to hang. The older guys had gone out of their way to take me along, so I felt a little bad about abandoning them to see Bob. But it would be fun to go "behind the scenes" at the store.

"Ice and me will go with him, keep him company," T-Jam said. "Cool?"

"Fully," D replied. "At the pizza place. Later."

He and Remo swaggered away toward the front of the mall. To be honest, I was relieved to see them go. Something told me that "hanging" wasn't all these guys were interested in. At least I *knew* T-Jam and Ice Box, and I could keep an eye on them.

As the three of us walked around the back of the mall, Bob looked up. His serious expression turned into a smile. "Hey, here come some of my favorite customers!"

With him were two men in khaki uniforms.

They gave us a bored look, then turned back to the clipboard.

Bob went over a few details with the men. Then they hopped onto the dock and opened the back of the truck.

"I still have your jazz tapes," Bob said to T-Jam. "You want them?"

T-Jam shook his head. "My dad says we have to bite the bullet. You know how it is."

"Sorry to hear that," Bob said. "I don't know where the kids get all this money to spend on Nicky Cash. Some of them buy four, five disks."

On the dock, the men were unloading cartons, almost all of them marked *Cash/Dreams of You*. Behind them was a storage area, with floor-to-ceiling shelves full of cassettes, records, and CDs. A half-open door led from the storage area into the store itself.

"Wow," Ice Box said. "What a stash."

"Come on up," Bob said. "I'll show you how the business works."

We climbed up. Bob pointed out different things on the shelves. Behind us, the truckers unloaded carton after carton. Finally they said to Bob, "Okay, we need your signature."

As Bob took their pen, T-Jam looked through the door into the store. "Whoa, Bob," he said, "something's going on in there."

Sure enough, we heard a couple of screams and some shouting.

Bob ran inside, followed by the two men, and then me. In the middle of the store, a crowd surrounded a woman who was gasping and clutching at her pocketbook. A man had put his arm around her, trying to calm her down.

Bob burst through the crowd, ran to her, and asked, "What happened, ma'am?"

"My — my purse!" she sputtered. "Someone tried to grab it from me."

"I saw him," a teenaged girl said. "He was really tall and had dark brown hair — "

"Dark red hair!" someone insisted.

"He had a mustache," somebody else called out.

People began shouting all at once. Everyone seemed to have a different opinion of what the guy looked like.

The crowd turned as two big guys in baseball caps ran breathlessly through the front door. They shrugged. "He's fast," one of them said. "He lost us right away."

I felt bad for that woman — and for Bob, too. I could tell he felt responsible.

At any rate, the last thing he needed was three thirteen-year-olds hanging around him. I looked behind me. T-Jam was nowhere to be seen, but Ice Box was standing in the half-open door to the storage area.

As I walked toward him, he called over his shoulder, "Yo, Jam!"

"Did you see that?" I asked.

"Nasty stuff," Ice Box said. I wanted to walk into the storage room and talk to T-Jam, but Ice wasn't moving.

"What's T-Jam doing?" I asked.

"I almost got him," came T-Jam's voice. He appeared behind Ice Box and pulled the door open all the way. "I saw some dude running into the parking lot. I thought it might be the one who tried to rip off the old lady. I went after him, but he drove away in a Jeep."

"You should report that to the police," I said.

"Squank," T-Jam answered. (I guess that means *no way* or something.) "I tell them anything, they suspect me. Now come on, let's book."

We hurried to the edge of the truck dock and jumped off. When we reached D's car, D was inside and Remo was standing by the open passenger door. The engine was running.

"Hey, what about the pizza place?" I asked as we crammed in the back.

Remo jumped in and slammed the door. D

stepped on the gas and tore away from the lot.

"We lost our appetite," Remo said.

I noticed he was sitting with his legs wide apart. I looked closer and saw a cardboard box at his feet.

A cardboard box labeled *Cash/Dreams of You*.

I froze. Thoughts tumbled around in my mind. There was only one place that box could have come from. But how could Remo have stolen it? Six of us had been watching the unloading of the shipment.

Until the woman started screaming. But then we *all* went inside —

No, T-Jam stayed in the truck dock — and Ice Box was standing in the door.

Standing guard.

It was dawning on me. The attempted theft was to distract us while T-Jam ripped off some disks. D and Remo *weren't* "hanging," after all. While one created the distraction, the other was helping T-Jam.

That was why we'd come to the mall. Because T-Jam had remembered about the shipment. And he knew Bob would trust us around the truck.

No. He knew Bob would trust *me*. T-Jam was using me. He had been using me all along.

I could see D's eyes glaring at me in the

rearview mirror. I felt sick to my stomach.

"You — you — " The words couldn't come out. I looked at T-Jam, but he just glanced away with a guilty smile. "Let me out. Now." I was surprised at the sound of my own voice. It was a low growl.

D slowed down and moved toward the curb. "It's a long walk," he said.

"I don't care. I don't care if I never see you guys again."

"Fine," D said as the car came to a stop. "But don't get any ideas about talking, dude."

Remo climbed out and pulled the seat forward. That leering grin was on his face. "You were part of this, Bruno boy. If we get caught, you go with us."

I felt dizzy. I looked at T-Jam.

He just shrugged. "Sorry, man. You're in about as deep as it gets."

CHAPTER 9

I don't remember the rest of that weekend. I know I managed to walk home. I know I ate two more meals on Saturday and three on Sunday. Other than that, it's all a blur.

I was a criminal. That was the thought that kept repeating in my head. Would Bob discover the theft? Of course he would. He had ordered a certain number of boxes. He knew how to count. And when he did, who was he going to blame?

Logan Bruno.

Bob's friendship with my dad would be out the window. Dad would be shocked. He would disown me, testify against me in court. Newspapers would show tearful photos of my parents saying things like, "He was such a nice boy. Where did we go wrong?"

On the evening news, people would watch me going to jail with a jacket over my head. "*He had it all,*" the voiceover would say, "*and he blew it on Nicky Cash and the Badd Boyz. Details at eleven."*

I couldn't sleep. I had nightmares about jail cells. I kept dreaming about the Badd Boyz, all laughing at me.

I was a basket case.

By Monday my head was starting to clear. I began to put things in perspective. Five to ten years, maybe. Not a life sentence.

Just kidding. But barely.

I walked to school that day feeling a little numb. A police car rolled down Kimball Street, and my stomach turned inside out. The car kept going, but I could taste my morning bacon for the next hour.

Fortunately Mary Anne had agreed to walk to school with Dawn. I wouldn't have wanted her to see me in my condition.

I had two more strokes of good luck. Neither the Badd Boyz nor the King Patrol were in front of the school. I could suffer my own personal meltdown in peace.

It wasn't until I opened my locker that I came back to reality.

Inside, hanging from a hook, was a black leather jacket with a Badd Boyz insignia on the back. Over the front pocket the name BRUNO was embroidered.

I was stunned. "What the — " I began to say.

"Like it? Bad, huh?"

I spun around. T-Jam was looking over my shoulder, admiring the coat.

"How did you get in my locker?" I demanded.

"Easy. We're buds, remember?" T-Jam said. "I've seen you open your locker a million times. Come on, don't you know your friends' combos by now, man?"

"No way!" I snapped. "It's none of my business. I wouldn't even think of — "

"Hey, all right, so I've got good eyesight. If you really didn't want to show me your combo, you could have blocked it off from me. But let's don't argue, okay? I brought you a leather jacket. What do you think?"

There were so many things I wanted to say. I started with the first thing that came to mind. "It looks . . . expensive. Where did you get it? *How* did you — "

"It was *au gratin*. That means free, if you taste my drift."

"You mean *gratis*," not caring if I sounded like a nerd, " — and you stole it, right? Who did you con into sewing my name?"

"Look, don't bring my mom into this. I thought you would be grateful. Do you know how many guys are dying to be one of us? And here I'm not only inviting you, I got you this coat. And I have to get yelled at?"

I yanked out the jacket and thrust it toward him. "I don't want it. Give it to somebody else, and take my name off."

"Your choice, Bruno. I'm trying hard not to be hurt. You better think about what you're doing, you know."

I felt a black hole forming in my mind. You know, like one of those places in outer space where the gravity is so strong it pulls in everything, including itself. Well, all my confused and tumbling thoughts were being pulled together. They were fitting into each other, starting to make some sense. I was suddenly not afraid anymore. I saw two clear choices ahead of me:

If I didn't tell anyone about Saturday, here's who would suffer: Bob Shull, all the future victims of the Badd Boyz, and me. Here's who *wouldn't* suffer: the Badd Boyz. And they'd have a kind of power over me, too. They could threaten to blackmail me, or just torment me the way T-Jam was doing then.

If I did tell, the Badd Boyz would be the ones who would suffer. And maybe they'd learn a lesson. Maybe they'd stop before their crimes became more serious. As for me? Well, I was *innocent*. That was the important thing. When innocent people tell the truth, justice takes care of them. (At least that's what's supposed to happen.)

"T-Jam," I said. "I *have* thought about it. I can't believe the way you used me. But I'll tell you what. If you return what you took from Sound Ideas, I won't get involved. If you don't, I'll go to . . ."

"Who?"

It was a good question. I hadn't thought of that one. "The . . . authorities."

I thought T-Jam was going to crack up. "The *authorities*? Like, the FBI? You're wiggy, Bruno. And I hope you're joking, because I know you won't even dream of ratting."

"Don't try to tell me I'm just as involved as you are."

T-Jam began counting on his fingers. (One.) "You led me and Ice to the shipment at the exact arrival time." (Two.) "When the lady started screaming in the store, you disappeared." (Three.) "You were in the storage room when the stuff was stolen." (Four.) "You didn't go back in and tell Bob anything, which you would have done, if you were innocent." (Five.) "Instead you ran straight to the getaway car. Plus, it's been two days and you still haven't contacted Bob." He grinned. "And you won't, because you are *el primo* suspect number one, Bruno baby."

Thwoop. My black hole was beginning to suck me right up.

T-Jam tossed the jacket over his shoulder.

"I'll hold on to this. Friends are important, man. And you're going to need some. You can't count on those muscleheads on the track team anymore. I can tell your girlfriend's not too happy, either. And how many other kids are going to want to hang with someone who steals Nicky Cash CDs?"

I could feel my face turning red. I opened my mouth, but nothing came out.

T-Jam sighed. His smile became a little more human. "Look, man, it's not so bad. These stores have insurance. D explained it to me. They get their money back, no sweat. Hey, we're small-time. Nobody's going to suffer. Meanwhile, we can sell some disks, make some cash on the side, and everybody's happy."

"Do it, then," I replied, "but leave me out."

T-Jam turned and walked away. "Just think about what I'm saying," he said over his shoulder. "You know what's good for you."

Needless to say, I was somewhere between a vegetable and the Walking Dead the rest of the day. Maybe it was my imagination, but I could swear people were crossing to the other side of the hall to avoid me. And I had remembered my deodorant that morning.

You know what the worst thing was? The Badd Boyz knew my locker combination, which meant I had no privacy. Any time they wanted, they could take something out or put something in.

That afternoon, before track, I opened my locker to find a note folded on the top shelf. I thought about throwing it out. I should have.

Instead, I picked it up and read it.

thiers more then one way to skin a rat!!!!

WATCH IT!

CHAPTER 10

T-Jam sounded shocked when I called him that night on the phone. "Pretty slimy. You know I would never do anything like that."

"Yeah? Then who did?" I demanded.

"Beats me, boss. Could be Skin — "

"*Skin?* If I see him tomorrow — "

"Whoa, gel, Bruno. I told you about Skin. He's got Rice Krispies for a brain — "

"That's no excuse!"

"Hey, listen up. I said *could be* Skin. Could be not. Look on the bright side. At least they didn't leave nothing in *her* locker."

"How do you know?"

"I *don't*! Look, man, all I know is that some of the guys are pretty upset about you saying you're going to rat on them."

"I *didn't* say that!"

"So you're not going to?"

I didn't have an answer to that. I paused and took a deep breath. "I haven't made up my mind. Maybe I'll just let you sweat it out the rest of the night."

" 'Cause I know you have to follow your conscience, but that note is some weird stuff. I mean, I'd hate it if whoever wrote that really *meant* something — "

Wham! I slammed the receiver down. I was steamed. Just when I'd thought they'd gone as low as they could, they proved me wrong. Threatening Mary Anne was scraping the bottom.

Well, I didn't call any authorities that night. Or the next night. I kept thinking of Mary Anne. Whoever had written that note *might* be crazy enough to do something to her — especially if it was Skin. If Mary Anne got hurt, I could never forgive myself.

Blackmail. That was what they called this kind of thing in the movies. And it was happening to normal old me.

All Tuesday, T-Jam kept giving me these thumbs-up gestures. Like, thanks for not ratting. I tried to avoid him. I even stayed in the library during lunch period.

Each time I went to my locker, I had a sinking feeling in my stomach. I tried to imagine what might be in there. A threat to my family? A warrant for my arrest?

Nothing. A normal locker the whole day.

Not until Wednesday morning did something strange appear on the top shelf. It was a long, narrow envelope covered with advertisements, the kind of envelope they give you when you buy tickets to sports events.

Great. The Badd Boyz were inviting me to a baseball game. I could just picture it. I'd be rooting for the home team while they were off stealing hot dogs.

I ripped open the envelope. A note was inside, wrapped around two tickets. First I read the note:

Thanks, Bruno. I
knew you'd understand.
Here's something you
might be able to use.
Enjoy. Jam

I looked at the tickets. They were for two seats at the Nicky Cash concert.

I had to look twice. Across all the newspaper ads for the concert were the words SOLD OUT. How could the Badd Boyz have gotten these?

I put my eyes right up to the tickets to see if they'd been forged. They sure looked real.

That meant either the Badd Boyz bought them long ago or they stole them, which narrowed my choices.

I wondered what poor girl was sobbing with

grief because of these tickets. There was no way I could use them. . . .

Still, I started imagining showing the tickets to Mary Anne. I could see the look on her face. Just the thought of it made me grin.

I put the tickets back on my shelf. I had to think about this some more.

During the day, the answer to the problem became clearer and clearer. I made the decision during the last period of the day. I couldn't accept the tickets. Not if they were illegal.

I walked to my locker, feeling depressed. Things hadn't been going well between Mary Anne and me. We hadn't seen each other all weekend, and I know she thought I was choosing the Badd Boyz over her. The tickets probably would have wiped out our problems.

I wanted to give the tickets back to T-Jam, but he wasn't in the hallway. That didn't surprise me. He usually left right after the final bell, without going to his locker. He didn't feel a need for books.

I figured I'd confront him the next day. I pulled open my locker and grabbed my jacket.

Just then a pair of hands reached around and covered my eyes.

"Surprise!"

I whirled around.

It was Mary Anne. "Ooh, I'm sorry. Did I scare you?"

"That's okay," I said. "Hi. What are you doing over here?"

She smiled. "I missed you. You don't mind, do you?"

"No! Are you kidding?"

Her eyes focussed on my locker shelf. "What's that?"

Panic. Sheer, blind panic. My locker door was all the way open, flush against the locker next to it. I reached behind me to grab it.

"Oh — uh, nothing," I said. "Just some, uh, baseball tickets."

"For us? Logan, that's so sweet. Can I see?" She reached toward the envelope. So did I.

Her hand got there first. I was sunk.

For a moment she didn't say a thing. Her eyes opened so wide I thought they'd fall out. Then her jaw dropped. "How — oh, I don't believe — this is so — "

Then she gave up trying to put it in words. Instead she threw her arms around me so hard I almost lost my balance.

"Oh, Logan, you are incredible!" she said. "The one thing I wanted more than anything else in the world! How did you get them?"

"Well, um . . ." (What could I say? I stood on line overnight? I found them in the gutter?) "I have my ways."

"I can't wait to show everybody! They will just drop! Which concert is it?" She read the ticket. "Friday. I'm sure my dad will let me go. Ohhhhhhh, I'm so happy!"

She hugged me again. I was stuck. The only thing I could do was make the best of it.

"You *have* to come to the BSC meeting today," she said. "Can you? It'll be so much fun to see the expressions on everybody's faces!"

"Sure," I said. "Why not?"

It would be fun. As long as no one paid attention to the look on *my* face.

After track I dragged myself to Claudia's house. Mary Anne was already there, looking as if she were about to explode.

The moment I walked in the door, she pulled out the tickets.

You would have thought Nicky Cash himself was in that envelope. Every single BSC member climbed onto the bed to see. I waited for it to collapse and send the club plunging into the Kishi's kitchen.

It didn't happen. Instead they left the bed and crowded around me. The questions flew fast and furious:

"Logan, how did you get them?"

"What are you guys going to wear?"

"Are you going to bring a camera?"

"Are you going to bring binoculars?"

"Can you get his autograph?"

I felt like a rock star myself, surrounded by fans. Fortunately, Kristy had her eye on the clock and called out, "This meeting will come to order!"

Dawn, Mary Anne, and Claudia reluctantly climbed back onto the bed. Stacey sat in Claud's desk chair, Kristy in the director's chair, and Mal and Jessi on the floor.

"Any new business?" Kristy asked.

"Yeah," Stacey said. "I move to give Logan a *medal*."

"I second!" Mary Anne cried.

"All in favor?" Kristy said.

"*Aye!*" everyone shouted.

"Okay, who's going to buy the medal?" Kristy asked.

"*You!*" they answered.

Everybody cracked up. Kristy arched her eyebrow.

Soon the phone started ringing. It was business as usual.

For the next half hour, the tickets were *almost* forgotten. Mal talked about how her younger siblings were being bugged by EJ. Stacey mentioned that Charlotte actually went to school wearing a helmet (I guess EJ was bopping her on the head). Dawn told us about an SMS student who thought a twenty-dollar bill had been taken from her purse, and Stacey reminded us about her wallet.

No reports of any tickets having been stolen. That was a relief.

I left the meeting a certified hero. Mary Anne didn't grill me about the Badd Boyz at all.

I was feeling better. I hoped it would stay that way.

CHAPTER 11

Thursday

Before I write about today, I just have to say: I HAVE THE WORLD'S BEST BOYFRIEND!!!!!

I am so psyched about tomorrow! Maybe I'll make a special entry in this book, just about the concert.

Earth to Mary Anne! We're supposed to write about our sitting experience, remember?

Oh, right. Sorry. Well, it was a pretty intense day. As usual, EJ was the main topic.

Topic? More like an obsession.

Mal, you sound frustrated.

Yeah. I have a house full of siblings who go to school with EJ.

Well, at least they've finally figured out a way to deal with him....

Mary Anne helped Mallory sit for her brothers and sisters Thursday after school. Now, Mal is a great sitter — and a great *sister*, I'm sure. But taking care of seven kids is no day at the beach.

Okay, you can't tell the players without a scorecard, so here's the roster of Pikes. After eleven-year-old Mallory, we skip a year but gain three kids. Translation: ten-year-old *triplets*. That's right, three boys named Adam, Byron, and Jordan. Next down the Pike pike is Vanessa, a nine-year-old girl who likes to talk in rhymes. Then there's Nicky, who's eight; Margo (seven); and Claire (five).

Actually, only Vanessa, Nicky, and Margo were the real EJ victims. Claire is only in kindergarten, and I guess the triplets were too old or too big for EJ.

The kids were in the backyard, playing freeze tag. Mal was interviewing Mary Anne for a report she was going to write called "A

Fan's Eyewitness Reaction to a Major Rock Concert."

"So, uh, when would you say your devotion to Mr. Fenster began?" Mal asked.

Mary Anne burst out laughing. "Mr. Fenster?"

"I'm trying to be official," Mal explained.

"Hi-iiii!"

Mary Anne and Mal looked up to see Marilyn and Carolyn skipping into the yard (the Arnolds live around the corner from the Pikes). "Hi, guys!" Mal called out.

As the twins joined the game, Mal grew serious again. "Now, how do you imagine you will feel about the performance?"

"Um, great, I think," Mary Anne said with a shrug.

"And what do you think it will be like to see the star in person?"

"Really exciting."

"And what kind of crowd do you think will be there?"

Mary Anne couldn't go on. She started giggling. "*Mal*, don't you think you should ask me this *after* the concert?"

"I'll ask you again afterward, Mary Anne. That way I'll see if it was as good as you expected — "

"Heeee-*yahhhh!*"

Mathew Hobart was announcing his arrival.

He was wearing a black Ninja uniform with all kinds of plastic weapons tucked into a belt. And he was swinging one of the weapons around while his older brother James rolled his eyes (James is eight and Mathew's six).

"He thinks he's going to protect us," James said.

"Don't forget, we're in this together," Vanessa said to Mathew.

"Hah! Hoo! Ho!" Mathew shifted from foot to foot, slashing the air with his hands.

Mary Anne and Mal looked at each other. "EJ?" Mary Anne asked.

Mal nodded. "EJ."

Before long Buddy Barrett arrived, then Haley Braddock. They're friends of the Pike kids (Buddy's eight and Haley's nine), and also charter members of the We Hate EJ Club.

The game of freeze tag soon stopped. The kids huddled at the edge of the yard, jabbering away.

"What are they doing?" Mary Anne asked Mal.

Mal shrugged. "It looks like they're declaring war. Maybe I should do my story on *this*."

Mary Anne didn't find it amusing. She walked over to the kids. "Uh, guys, what are you up to?"

"Nothing," Nicky snapped.

"We're uniting, like the United States!" Vanessa blurted out.

"Yeah," Buddy echoed. "Together we'll be strong!"

"Bully or no bully," Haley said. "EJ is just *one person!*"

Behind Mary Anne, the triplets barged out of the house. "Look!" Adam shouted. "It's the Scaredy Cats!"

"*Adammm,*" Mary Anne warned sternly. Then she turned back to the younger kids and said, "You know, ganging up on somebody isn't fair — "

"We're not ganging up!" Margo insisted.

"We're just going to stick together," Buddy explained, "in *groups*. Like, walking to school, and at lunchtime, and walking home. That way, EJ can't bully us anymore!"

"Yeah," Haley said. "We're stronger than EJ!"

"I *hope* so!" Jordan mumbled. The triplets burst into giggles.

This time Mal spoke up. "I guess you guys are too big and tough to be bullied by EJ, huh?"

Adam, Jordan, and Byron smirked at each other. "Uh . . . yeah, I guess so," Adam said, as if that were the dumbest question ever asked.

"So how come you haven't been protecting

your brothers and sisters from him?" Mal went on.

The triplets started laughing. "Mal," Adam said. "EJ is — "

"*Adam, don't!*" Vanessa screamed.

"Oh, come *on*," Jordan moaned.

Nicky's lip was quivering. "You *promised*."

"I'll never let you use my Game Boy," Buddy said.

That did the trick. The triplets backed off. "Let's get away from these babies," Jordan said.

Vanessa gave Mary Anne and Mal a sharp look. "Now, would you *please*. . . ." She made a shooing motion with her hand. "We're having a stragedy session."

Mary Anne and Mal walked back toward the house. "*Stragedy?*" Mary Anne whispered with a smile.

"What do you think their big secret is?" Mal asked.

"Who knows? It sounds like EJ's doing something really embarrassing to them."

Mal looked back at the kids. They were practically jumping with excitement. "Well, maybe he won't bother them so much after today." She picked up her legal pad from the stoop. "Okay, let's finish. Now, what do you think your favorite song will be?"

Well, Mary Anne survived the interview,

and the sitting job. She called me that night, excited about the kids' new plans. They had worked out a schedule of who was going to walk with whom, always making sure to stay in groups of four or more. They also figured out elaborate routes to school, so they could pick up as many kids as possible on the way.

"I'm so proud of them," Mary Anne said. "They decided how to deal with EJ without any fighting."

"And they thought of it by themselves," I replied.

"I know! You should have heard Mathew explaining 'strength in numbers' to me. He kept saying, 'Two is stronger than one, three is stronger than two, four is stronger than three. . . .' "

Strength in numbers. It was a great idea.

I should know. It was being used against me.

CHAPTER 12

"Hey, it's okay if you don't have the guts, G-Man. Everyone else does."

I could hear T-Jam's unmistakable voice around the corner of the school. It was Friday afternoon and I'd just come out of the door from the gym to the parking lot. I was dressed in my sweats, ready for practice. To reach the field, I had to walk around the corner wall. But the last person I wanted to see was T-Jam.

All week long I'd been following my own "stragedy" to avoid the Badd Boyz. It wasn't too hard, considering they all stuck together. I just made sure to take different hallway routes than they did.

I figured they'd given up on me. T-Jam wasn't throwing me thumbs-up signs anymore. He wasn't even saying hello. It was as if I'd never gotten involved with them.

They had bought my silence with those tickets. I was sure that's how they felt.

Near the corner was a huge Dumpster with an open top. I sidled into the narrow space between it and the wall.

"I do have the guts," G-Man said. "I just don't think it's going to be as easy as the last time. Unless we take Ken Doll with us."

Ken Doll?

"We don't need him," T-Jam said. "Look, I was in the store yesterday. The owner thinks I'm, like, a regular customer. He tells me everything. Anyway, the truck's coming in the same time on Saturday. All we do is hang out. The store will be crowded. It'll be like last week. He'll leave some boxes on the dock while he goes in and out of the door. And when he goes *in*. . . ."

"Wham! We grab."

That was Ice Box's voice. They were walking slowly past the Dumpster now. I huddled as far into the shadows as I could.

"We only do it if it's fully safe," T-Jam said. "We watch before we do anything stupid. The important thing is *positioning*. Two of us'll be in Remo's dad's car, you know, lying on the floor and peeking. Two more will hang out by the corner of the building."

"What about Remo?" Ice Box asked. "Is he going to go after some poor old lady again? That was sick."

"Nah, D pounded him about that," T-Jam answered. "Said it was too risky. Better to keep it simple and safe."

As they walked away, I lost track of what they were saying. But it didn't matter. I had heard enough. They were going to rob Sound Ideas again.

I had to do something about it — but what? If I called Bob, he'd keep an eye on the boxes. But something inside of me wanted the Badd Boyz to get caught. Maybe I should call the cops. But what about my part in all this? What about T-Jam's threats?

I could hear Coach Leavitt's whistle on the field. I jogged over to him, completely confused.

One thing was sure. This had to stop. Whether or not I was *legally* guilty of anything, I was the Badd Boyz' connection to Sound Ideas, so Saturday was going to be on my shoulders. I couldn't stay quiet anymore.

Especially not with a bunch of yahoos who would call me *Ken Doll*.

They were going to regret that.

That night was the Nicky Cash concert. I tried to block out how weird I felt about those tickets. After track, I ran home, dressed in my nicest clothes, put on some cologne (which I hate to do), and went to the BSC meeting.

"Gag me!" Kristy shouted when I walked in.

"*Stop*," Mary Anne said. "I think he smells nice!"

"Me too," Dawn agreed.

"The beetig of the Baby-sitters Club will cub to order!" Kristy announced, pinching her nose.

(See the abuse I put up with? Actually, I'll take that to being called Ken Doll anytime.)

The meeting whizzed by. I have to say, I couldn't keep my eyes off Mary Anne. She was wearing this incredibly sexy outfit with sequins on it (yes, *Mary Anne*). Not a dress but a shirt and pants that are attached, whatever that's called.

I'd never seen Mary Anne so excited. She actually booked Jessi for two different jobs at the same time. Fortunately Jessi realized it immediately and they were able to change things around.

Now that is *really* not like Mary Anne.

When the meeting was over, we went downstairs together. Charlie Thomas was waiting to take Kristy home, and he'd agreed to drop off Mary Anne and me in downtown Stoneybrook. We were going to have dinner at a fancy restaurant, and then my dad would pick us up and drive us to Stamford for the concert. (Mary Anne's dad was paying for dinner. I told you he was a nice guy.)

" 'Bye!" Claudia, Dawn, Stacey, Mal, and Jessi squealed as we climbed into the Junk Bucket (that's the name of Charlie's car, and for good reason)."Tell us all about it!"

With a few clanks and coughs, the Junk Bucket took off. "Where to?" Charlie asked.

"Renwick's," I said.

"We're having a candlelight dinner!" Mary Anne added.

Charlie moved his eyebrows up and down a couple of times. "Hmmm, a candlelight dinner?"

"Yeah. Charlie, have you ever tasted candlelight?" Kristy said. "It's magnificent."

"Kristy!" Mary Anne threw her head back and laughed.

" 'Yes, waiter, we'll have the candlelight dinner for two,' " Kristy said, imitating a restaurant customer. " 'Make my candlelight medium rare — and you, dear?' "

"Well done!" Mary Anne said.

"Thank you!" Kristy replied.

By the time we arrived at the restaurant we were all laughing, even Charlie.

When the Junk Bucket rattled away, I could see a few of the Renwick's ritzy customers looking a little . . . shocked.

We didn't care. It was a cool, clear night,

the food smells were making our mouths water, and Mary Anne looked fantastic. The waiter led us to a table in a romantic corner by a small waterfall.

In the pool below the waterfall were a million or so coins. Mary Anne reached into her purse, took out a penny, and threw it in.

"What did you wish?" I asked.

"That we will have many, many more times as wonderful as this," Mary Anne answered.

Hoo boy. I melted. Her eyes were so warm, and so full of trust.

I should have felt great. Mary Anne was happy. We were going to see her very favorite singer. We were having a free restaurant dinner. And there was no school the next day.

But I kept thinking about the conversation I'd overheard at school. I couldn't shake it from my mind. And that made me think of the tickets again.

You've already gone this far, Bruno, I told myself. *There's no turning back.* I tried to smile and be happy, for Mary Anne's sake.

We ordered. The waiter served salad, then the main course (pasta for Mary Anne, T-bone steak for me). I was proud of myself. I thought I was making excellent conversation, with no trace of guilt.

Then Mary Anne said, "You did bring the tickets, right?"

I pulled them out of my pocket. "Sure did."

"Whew. Because, you know, stuff has been disappearing around school these days. Even tickets. You heard about Anne Kennedy."

"No," I said. "I don't know her."

Mary Anne's brow furrowed. "She's this seventh-grader. One of the people whose locker was broken into."

"And someone took her tickets?"

"You didn't hear about this? Anne was sobbing for hours! Whoever it was just took the tickets and nothing else."

My mouth felt like sandpaper. "Wow . . . when did it happen?"

"Hmm . . . Tuesday or Wednesday?" She thought about it a few seconds. "Yeah, it must have been then. She was absent those days and left them in her locker, so she found out yesterday."

"Oh."

Sobbing. The girl who was supposed to have these tickets was devastated. Why hadn't I heard about it? Because I'd been spending so much time avoiding everybody. I hadn't wanted to face Mary Anne, since I felt guilty about the Badd Boyz. I was walking around in my own cocoon.

And now I was taking Mary Anne to Anne Kennedy's concert.

I dropped my fork onto my plate. A minute

ago I had torn into the juiciest steak I had ever tasted. Now I might as well have been looking at a piece of chalk.

It was time to stop feeling weird and guilty and sheepish and phony and whatever else was running around in my brain. It was time to do the right thing.

Finally.

"Mary Anne," I said with a sigh. "I don't know how to say this, but we're not going to the concert tonight."

CHAPTER 13

He's joking. He's not joking. He's being weird. He's serious.

In about two seconds, those were the expressions that went across Mary Anne's face.

"Logan, what do you mean?"

Squank! Just kidding. Let's go! a voice inside me wanted to say. It killed me to see Mary Anne's mood burst apart like this.

"We can't use these tickets," I said. "I — I didn't buy them, Mary Anne. They're not mine."

"Well, whose are they?"

"I don't know for sure. All I can tell you is that T-Jam gave them to me."

I could see the color drain from Mary Anne's face.

"I don't know where he got them," I went on. "He didn't tell me a thing."

"Oh, no." Mary Anne's voice was little more

than a whisper. She looked as though she were in a trance.

"I was going to talk to T-Jam about the tickets. But you saw them before I had a chance, and I couldn't bear to take them back. If I had known about Anne Kennedy — "

"But Logan, where did you *think* T-Jam got those tickets? You know the Badd Boyz are stealing tons of stuff in school."

I am one of the few people who have seen Mary Anne Spier get angry. It doesn't happen very often. Sometimes it's hard to see it coming.

It wasn't hard now. Her face was turning red. Her eyes were narrow and cold.

"I can't believe we're sitting here, laughing and eating and being so romantic, when Anne is probably crying her heart out. And all because of your stupid, selfish, horrible friends!"

She pushed back her chair and stood up. I thought she was going to dump a glass of water on my head. Instead she began walking away.

"Where are you going?" I asked.

"To a pay phone. I'm going to call Anne right now."

I sat there, slumped in my chair, feeling like a total jerk. But I had said what I needed to say. I hadn't just used the tickets.

Mary Anne returned about five minutes

later. She wouldn't even look at me when she sat down.

"Did you get her?" I asked.

"Yes. She was so happy, she screamed. Her mom is driving her here right now, and we are going to give her the tickets. I didn't tell her all the details. I'll leave that to you." She shook her head, as if that would tame the anger that was bucking around inside. "Why did you do it, Logan? Why? If the concert was sold out, it was sold out. Did you think I wanted to go so badly that you had to get those . . . *thieves* involved?"

I let out a breath. My eyes were beginning to well up. "Mary Anne," I said, "I didn't ask T-Jam to get me those tickets. He gave them to me. I found them in my locker Wednesday morning."

"You let him have your combination? *I* don't even know your combination. I guess you guys are real close, huh? He likes you so much he steals tickets for you and delivers them right to your locker. What a friend!"

"No! No, Mary Anne. It's not like that at all. He sneaked a look at my combination when I was opening my locker. I didn't know it. And the tickets . . . well, the tickets were a bribe, I guess. To make sure I didn't rat on the Badd Boyz for something they did last Saturday. . . ."

Mary Anne sat back in her seat. The rage was draining from her face and she was looking intently at me. *Go on*, her expression said.

I explained it all. From the very beginning. How T-Jam stuck up for me in front of King, how the Badd Boyz made me feel welcome, the events that led up to the robbery at Sound Ideas. Finally I told her about the horrible note that threatened her.

When I got to that part, Mary Anne's eyes misted over. "I can't believe they did that to you, Logan. They are so cruel."

I swallowed a lump in my throat. What a feeling it was to be able to *talk* about this. It was as if I'd been carrying around steel shoulder pads for a week and someone had yanked them off. "Mary Anne, I was so . . . confused."

"And scared," she said gently.

"Yeah. Scared. I could be in real trouble. And I'm worried that they might try to do something to you."

Mary Anne reached across the table. She put her hands on mine.

I felt something warm trickle down my cheek.

"You have to tell your parents," Mary Anne said. "You know you do."

I nodded. "Yeah. I know."

Mary Anne looked up. She saw someone

come in, and she waved. I quickly wiped my face with my napkin.

"Where are they?" a voice squealed behind me.

I took the tickets from my pocket and turned. A pretty red-haired girl was looking at me as if I were Santa Claus. "Here you go," I said.

She grabbed them so fast they almost ripped. Then she threw her arms around me. "Oooooh, thank you! Thank you! I don't know how I can . . . thank you!"

I couldn't help but smile. "You're welcome. Don't be late!"

"Okay! 'Bye, Mary Anne! 'Bye, um . . ."

"Logan."

"Yeah! Oh, I'm sooooo happy! I'll tell you about it in school . . . whoa!"

She almost collided with a bus boy before she was swallowed up by the revolving door. We watched her jump into a car, which then sped away toward Stamford.

"I hope that was Anne Kennedy," I said.

Mary Anne laughed. "It was."

"Well, that was Good Deed Number One," I said.

Suddenly our appetites had come roaring back. We tore into our pasta and steak (slightly cold now), and had one of the best dinners in our lives.

My dad picked us up right on time. He hopped out of the car to open the door for Mary Anne (he's like that), and smiled at us. "Well, you two sure look ready for the concert."

"We're going home, Dad," I said. "I'll explain when we get there. It's a long story."

My long story was much easier to tell with Mary Anne to help me. We sat around the living room, drinking iced tea. Dad and Mom listened patiently, except every once in a while I could see my dad's upper lip pull back a little. Then he'd smack his right fist into his left palm.

"Logan, those boys sound awful," Mom said.

"I knew some fellows like that in high school," Dad commented. "But such behavior at this age. . . ." He pounded his palm again.

"I think it was courageous of you to admit everything," Mom said.

"You bet," Dad agreed. "It takes a man to admit he made a mistake — and a good man to try to make it better."

Now that's the kind of corny saying I would usually roll my eyes at. But at the moment I felt moved. I thought Dad was going to be mad, but he wasn't. I could tell he was proud of me.

"Now I want to do something about it. Is . . . the police station open?"

Dad smiled. "Twenty-four hour service. Come on, one of us will drive you. We can drop off Mary Anne on the way."

"No, I'd like to come, too," Mary Anne said.

"Okay, more support can't hurt."

Mom decided to stay at home with Kerry and Hunter. So Dad, Mary Anne, and I drove to the Stoneybrook Police.

There, we met a police sergeant named Bridget Ianelli, who calmly filled out a form while I told my story *again*.

"Don't worry, Mr. Bruno," Sergeant Ianelli said when she finished. (I thought she was talking to Dad, but she was looking at me.) "We'll have an unmarked car in that lot at nine forty-five tomorrow morning. You can be sure that if anything happens, we'll catch the boys in the act."

"Super," Dad said. "Thank you."

"Yeah, thanks," I added.

"And I wouldn't worry about those threats," Officer Ianelli said to Mary Anne. "I'll assign some officers to look out for you for a few days, just as a precaution. But I'll be honest with you. We've had some experience with these guys. They often make this kind of threat, and they never act on it. I've seen versions of that rat note for years. Last year one kid was really shaken up by it. Some boy named Dennis. You might know him."

"Skin . . ." I said under my breath. It was hard to imagine him in my shoes.

Officer Ianelli stood up. My dad grimly shook her hand. So did Mary Anne and I.

"Before you all go, I'd like to talk with you a minute, young man," she said to me. She turned to Dad. "May I?"

"Sure," Dad replied.

She took me to an inner office and sat me down. "I'll be brief. I know some of these kids. A couple of the older ones have been here a few times. Some of the younger ones'll be in here, too, guaranteed. *Some.* A lot of them straighten out. But you know what? I remember all of them when they first started. They're not unlike you, Logan. Do you catch what I'm saying?"

I nodded. "I sure do."

"Good." She smiled. "Now get out of here. I hope I never see you again."

CHAPTER 14

"*Dreeeeeams of yoooooooou . . .*"

Guess who woke me up on Saturday morning? Nicky Cash.

No, he wasn't making a personal appearance at the Bruno household. But his voice was. My sister, little Kerry Bruno, had become the latest American girl to lose her heart to Reginald Fenster.

"Would you please turn that down?" I, Draculogan, yelled.

"*Night and da-ay, day and ni-ight . . .*"

I hobbled out of bed. I retracted my fangs. I creaked to the top of the stairs. "Would you please turn that down?" I repeated.

"*These dreeeeeams of yoooooooou . . .*"

Now Kerry was singing along. I stomped downstairs.

There she was, lying on the couch. A huge smile was on her face and she was hugging the CD box.

"Uh, Kerry?"

She looked at me, but as if I weren't there. Finally I turned the volume down.

"Hey!" she cried, leaping off the couch.

"It's too loud," I said. "It's also too early. You know, we *do* have headphones."

"Ohhhh, you're so mean."

She plopped back on the couch, and I went into the kitchen. I scrambled some eggs, to the rhythm of what was becoming my least favorite song of all time.

As I ate, Mom, Dad, and Hunter straggled into the kitchen one at a time. Hunter didn't seem to mind the music, but I could tell Dad wasn't especially thrilled about it. "This was what you were going to hear last night?" he asked.

I almost spit out my eggs laughing. "Pretty terrible, huh?"

"*Stop!*" Kerry called from the living room.

We ate our breakfasts, trying to ignore the noise. At one point, Dad looked at the clock and said, "It won't be long now, I guess."

It was nine-thirty. The police car would be pulling into the parking lot soon. I felt creepy. Even though the Badd Boyz had been jerks, I felt as if I were betraying them. I also wasn't sure the scheme would work. Those guys might see the police and back off. *We only do it if it's fully safe*, T-Jam had said.

Mom knew what I was thinking. "Don't worry, Logan, you did the right thing."

"Yeah," Hunter said, his mouth full of Froot Loops, "you did."

"How do you know?" I asked.

Hunter shrugged and shoved in another spoonful. "You always do."

I laughed. But his words stuck in my mind. From now on, I would certainly try to live up to those expectations.

Later that day, Dad got a call from Bob Shull. The police had picked up D, Remo, T-Jam, Ice Box, Skin, and Butcher Boy. After they had been driven away, Sergeant Ianelli had stayed to tell Bob the whole story.

Dad put me on the phone in the middle of the call.

"Thanks, Logan," Bob said. "It must have been hard to tell on your pals. You know, I was a little suspicious of those guys when you first came in with them. But I figured if they were your friends. . . ."

"Yeah," I said. "I know what you mean. I'm sorry."

"It's okay," he said with a chuckle. "Not all of my boyhood friends turned out as magnificent as me."

I hung out with Mary Anne a lot the rest of the weekend. She told me the members of the

BSC had been really worried about me. One of them had even proposed that they "nullify my membership" because I might be "a bad influence on the kids." (She wouldn't tell me who said that, but I had a feeling it was Kristy.)

It was a rough week at school. Kids were acting really weird toward me. I realized they had been doing that for a while. I guess I'd been so caught up in my problems that I was oblivious to everything else.

At lunch on Monday, I sat with Trevor Sandbourne, Austin Bentley, and Lew Greenberg. They're all good friends (Lew is one of the *good* guys on the track team). They were pretty cold to me at first, but I ended up telling them what had happened. I told them everything.

"Wow," Aus said. "We thought you went hoody on us."

"Not me," Trevor said. "I figured it was, like, temporary insanity. I knew it wasn't really you."

Lew nodded. "I don't know, sometimes I think it might be kind of fun to hang out with those dudes."

"Get out of here!" Aus said.

"Uh-oh, Greenberg the Greaser!" Trevor added.

"No, I mean, I'm not saying I *would* do it,"

Lew insisted. "But, you know, don't you guys ever feel like being *bad* once in awhile — just in a fantasy?"

Aus and Trevor grumbled disagreement. But I knew what Lew meant. I guess I wasn't the only one who'd felt that way.

I also saw Jackhammer a couple of times that week. He wouldn't look me in the eye. I could tell he was furious. All his friends were gone.

Which leads me to the strangest thing of all. The other Badd Boy who was not picked up was G-Man. Well, on Monday he was pretty nasty, like Jackhammer. But on Tuesday he showed up without his Badd Boyz jacket, and he didn't wear it the rest of the week. By Friday he was hanging out with kids I'd never seen him with before. I actually saw him smile a few times.

As for T-Jam and his gang, they went to juvenile court and had to pay a fine. They were also suspended from school. The story was written up in the local newspaper. Their names weren't mentioned because of their age — but D and Remo *were* mentioned, so everyone at SMS could figure out who the others were.

Another thing happened that week. The thefts around school stopped. Girls let their bags hang from their shoulders, instead of clutching them to their chests.

You could actually feel everyone in school breathing easier.

I started getting more involved with track practice. I noticed King was really moody and quiet all week. Finally, after practice on Friday, he sat down next to me in the locker room and grunted hi.

Yes, *the* Clarence King.

"Yo, Logan," he said. "Did you really rat on those guys?"

"Yeah," I replied. "What about it?"

I expected some dumb comment. Instead he just stared at the floor for awhile and then said, "That took some guts, man."

I thought I was going to fall off the bench in disbelief. "Yeah? You think so?"

King nodded. "I mean, you were stupid to be their friend, that's for sure. But you really got them. . . ." His voice trailed off. "I couldn't do it."

"Huh?"

"Remember that fight I had with Jackhammer? When I almost killed him?"

That wasn't the way *I* remembered it. But I said, "Yeah . . ."

"Well, back then they wanted me to join them, too. And I didn't know much about them. I guess they looked okay or something, so I hung with them — but only for a couple of days. Then they started doing some stupid

126

stuff. We were at this store and Jackhammer took a little radio. The clerk noticed it was missing from the counter and he yelled at *me*. We all ran away, and afterward was when I got into that fight." He exhaled heavily. "I was really mad. I told T-Jam I was going to blow them open about the robberies they were doing. *He* said he and his buddies would say *I* was the thief. And then those grease monkeys left me a note saying they were going to go after my little brother. Anyway, *that* was why I never fought back later when T-Jam was ranking on me. I could have creamed that little twerp. But he had my number, if you know what I mean."

I looked at King. For the first time in my life I registered a human feeling about him other than disgust. "Yeah," I said. "It sounds like what happened to me."

King stood up. "Oh, well. Now that you got smart, maybe you'll stop being such a spazz on the field."

With that familiar idiot grin, he walked away.

I smiled. *Now* my life was returning to normal.

CHAPTER 15

"Order!" Kristy said at the precise click of 5:30 on the clock.

"BLT on rye toast!" I called out.

"Oh, you're going to get it, Logan." Kristy wagged her pencil at me. "I knew those guys were a bad influence on you."

It was Monday, a week and two days after the Capture of the Badd Boyz. The Baby-sitters Club had decided not to kick me out (although I'll bet Kristy was having second thoughts).

"Any new business?" Kristy asked.

"Dues!" Stacey piped up.

"Doones!" Claudia said, pulling out a package of Lorna Doones. She passed them around while everyone coughed up their dues money. (Under her bed was a bag of flourless, yeastless, sugarless, and probably tasteless "walnut fudgie bars" for Dawn and Stacey. I would hate to read the ingredient list on those.)

"Okay, next order of business is the recent

development in the ongoing EJ predicament," Kristy announced.

"*Kristy*," Claudia said. "Speak English."

"I thought I was," Kristy said with a smile. "And very well, thank you."

There *had* been some pretty amazing developments over the week. The kids' plan had worked! They had stuck to their groups every day. EJ was powerless. The thefts and threats just stopped.

Everyone in the BSC knew that. But today something new happened. Only Mal, Jessi, and I had heard about it, because our siblings were members of Anti-EJ groups.

"Okay, I'll start," Jessi said. "Becca was walking home from school today with some of her friends. EJ saw them and started making fun of them — saying, 'Sissies, sissies,' and 'What's the matter, too chicken to fight me alone?' and stuff like that. Anyway, then they decided to — "

"Don't forget 'Cross this line,' " Mal interrupted.

"Oh, right!" Jessi said. "One of the things EJ usually does is draw an imaginary line on the sidewalk and say, 'I dare you to cross this line!' And the kids always stop and cry, or cross the street."

"Or get into a fight, if they do cross the line," Mal added.

"Well, this time EJ drew the line in front of them," Jessi continued. "And you know what they did? All of them — Becca, Kerry, Charlotte, Mathew, and James — linked arms and walked over the line. Together. With their chins held high."

"Yea!" Claudia started applauding.

"What happened then?" Kristy asked.

"EJ burst into tears," Jessi answered. "Just broke down and cried like a baby."

"You're kidding!" Stacey exclaimed.

"Wait! That's only the beginning!" Mal said. "Logan should tell you what happened after that."

"Okay," I replied. "Well, Kerry said she felt bad. She hates to see anybody cry, except Hunter. So she went and invited EJ to our house. Anyway, the other kids thought she was crazy. But Kerry put her arm around EJ's shoulder, and EJ just came along, as peaceful as a kitten."

"Were you there when they got home?" Dawn asked. "Did you see what he looked like?"

"Uh . . . yes and no. I *was* home, but I didn't see what he looked like."

"Huh?" Claudia said.

"I didn't see him," I went on, "because he is a she. EJ's name is Eleanor Jane."

For a long moment you could hear the clock

buzzing. Five mouths hung open. I wished I had some popcorn for target practice.

Finally Mary Anne said, "EJ is a *girl*?"

Dawn laughed. "Well, hey, why not? Girls can be as nasty as boys. I mean, it's kind of sexist to think only boys can be bullies."

"Or that only girls can be baby-sitters," I added.

"That's for sure," Mary Anne agreed.

"It's the same with doctors," Stacey said. "Charlotte's mom says that when people hear the name Dr. Johanssen they assume she's a man. People think all nurses are female, too. There are three male nurses on the staff, and patients always call them 'Doctor.' "

"I hope King never has to be hospitalized," I remarked. "I could just picture him calling out, 'Hey, nurse, where's your purse?' "

"No way," Kristy said. "It wouldn't happen. You need a brain to make up a rhyme."

"Maybe someday there will be equality," I said. "And people will realize that girls can be stupid jocks, too."

Claudia pelted me with a Lorna Doone.

"Squank!" Kristy yelled.

Mary Anne pushed me off the bed.

"Feed him a walnut fudgie bar!" Dawn shouted.

"No! No! Anything but that!"

The meeting dissolved into a festival of giggles. It would have totally degenerated, but Mrs. Hobart called to set up a sitting job, and a couple of other calls followed soon after.

Remember I said that I sometimes feel awkward at BSC meetings? Not at that one. I was having a good time. In fact, I hadn't felt so good in weeks.

And it wasn't only for the reasons you think. I had something up my sleeve. Since Friday I'd felt bad that Mary Anne had to miss the concert. I'd called the box office just to make sure Nicky Cash wasn't coming back to Stamford.

Well, he wasn't. But the ticket agent told me the tour schedule for the next few weeks: Boston, Albany, Atlanta, Pittsburgh, Philadelphia, and New York City.

And you know me. Ready to take the bull by the horns.

After the meeting, I strolled outside with Mary Anne. We said good-bye to everyone, and I offered to walk home with her.

The sun was just starting to set as we walked along Burnt Hill Road. I reached into my pocket as if I'd just remembered something. "Oh!" I said. "You think your dad would let you go to New York City with me?"

Now, Mary Anne *loves* New York City. She wants to live there when she grows up. "Sure!" she said, her eyes lighting up. "I mean, if he went with us. Or if we went with Stacey to see her father or something."

"Hmmmm," I said. "Well, I only have two tickets." I pulled them out and held them toward her.

Mary Anne stopped in her tracks. She took the tickets and read: " 'Nicky Cash. Radio City Music Hall.' Logan, where — how did you get these?"

"Oh, I found them in my locker."

Her face fell. She gave me a Look. *"Logannn . . ."*

"NOT!" I said.

"Did you?"

"No, Mary Anne! I really, seriously bought them and picked them up at a real, live ticket outlet. Do you want to go?"

I thought she was going to fly off into the sunset. Instead she just put her arms around me. *"Do* I?" Oh, Logan, you are the best! *Thank you!"* She planted a kiss on my cheek. Then she started crying on my shoulder.

It was a little embarrassing, out there in the middle of the sidewalk.

But I could deal with it.

About the Author

ANN M. MARTIN did *a lot* of baby-sitting when she was growing up in Princeton, New Jersey. She is a former editor of books for children, and was graduated from Smith College.

Ms. Martin lives in New York City with her cats, Mouse and Rosie. She likes ice cream and *I Love Lucy*; and she hates to cook.

Ann Martin's Apple Paperbacks include *Yours Turly, Shirley*; *Ten Kids, No Pets*; *With You and Without You*; *Bummer Summer*; and all the other books in the Baby-sitters Club series.

THE BABY-SITTERS CLUB ®

by Ann M. Martin

More titles... ▶

❑ MG44970-2	#49 Claudia and the Genius of Elm Street	$3.25
❑ MG44969-9	#50 Dawn's Big Date	$3.25
❑ MG44968-0	#51 Stacey's Ex-Best Friend	$3.25
❑ MG44966-4	#52 Mary Anne + 2 Many Babies	$3.25
❑ MG44967-2	#53 Kristy for President	$3.25
❑ MG44965-6	#54 Mallory and the Dream Horse	$3.25
❑ MG44964-8	#55 Jessi's Gold Medal	$3.25
❑ MG45657-1	#56 Keep Out, Claudia!	$3.25
❑ MG45658-X	#57 Dawn Saves the Planet	$3.25
❑ MG45659-8	#58 Stacey's Choice	$3.25
❑ MG45660-1	#59 Mallory Hates Boys (and Gym)	$3.25
❑ MG45662-8	#60 Mary Anne's Makeover	$3.50
❑ MG45663-6	#61 Jessi's and the Awful Secret	$3.50
❑ MG45664-4	#62 Kristy and the Worst Kid Ever	$3.50
❑ MG45665-2	#63 Claudia's Friend Friend	$3.50
❑ MG45666-0	#64 Dawn's Family Feud	$3.50
❑ MG45667-9	#65 Stacey's Big Crush	$3.50
❑ MG45575-3	Logan's Story Special Edition Readers' Request	$3.25
❑ MG44240-6	Baby-sitters on Board! Super Special #1	$3.95
❑ MG44239-2	Baby-sitters' Summer Vacation Super Special #2	$3.95
❑ MG43973-1	Baby-sitters' Winter Vacation Super Special #3	$3.95
❑ MG42493-9	Baby-sitters' Island Adventure Super Special #4	$3.95
❑ MG43575-2	California Girls! Super Special #5	$3.95
❑ MG43576-0	New York, New York! Super Special #6	$3.95
❑ MG44963-X	Snowbound Super Special #7	$3.95
❑ MG44962-X	Baby-sitters at Shadow Lake Super Special #8	$3.95
❑ MG45661-X	Starring the Baby-sitters Club Super Special #9	$3.95

Available wherever you buy books...or use this order form.

Scholastic Inc., P.O. Box 7502, 2931 E. McCarty Street, Jefferson City, MO 65102

Please send me the books I have checked above. I am enclosing $——————
(please add $2.00 to cover shipping and handling). Send check or money order - no cash or C.O.D.s please.

Name ——————————————————————————————————————

Address ————————————————————————————————————

City—————————————— State/Zip ——————————————

Please allow four to six weeks for delivery. Offer good in the U.S. only. Sorry, mail orders are not available to residents of Canada. Prices subject to change.

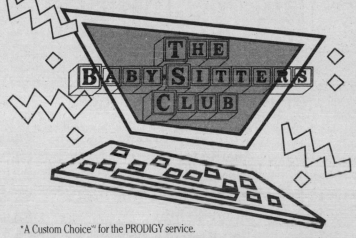